# the other city

Originally published in Czech as *Druhé město* by Mladá fronta, 1993
Copyright © Michal Ajvaz, 1993
Translation copyright © Gerald Turner, 2009
First English translation, 2009
Second printing, 2011
All rights reserved

Library of Congress Cataloging-in-Publication Data

Ajvaz, Michal, 1949-
[Druhé mesto. English]
The other city / Michal Ajvaz ; translated by Gerald Turner.
p. cm.
ISBN 978-1-56478-491-9 (pbk. : acid-free paper)
I. Turner, Gerald. II. Title.
PG5039.1.J83D7813 2009
891.8'635--dc22
2009001365

Partially funded by grants from the National Endowment for the Arts, a federal agency; the Illinois Arts Council, a state agency; and by the University of Illinois at Urbana-Champaign.

This translation was subsidized by the Ministry of Culture of the Czech Republic.

www.dalkeyarchive.com
Cover: design by Danielle Dutton, illustration by Nicholas Motte
Printed on permanent/durable acid-free paper and bound in the United States of America

# the other city
# a novel by michal ajvaz

Translated by Gerald Turner

Dalkey Archive Press
Champaign and London

# Chapter 1
## The Book with the Purple Binding

I was walking up and down the rows of books at the antiquarian bookseller's in Karlova Street. Now and then I would take a look out the shop window. It started to snow heavily; holding a book in my hand I watched the snowflakes swirling in front of the wall of St Savior's Church. I returned to my book, savoring its aroma and allowing my eyes to flit over its pages, reading here and there the fragment of a sentence that suddenly sparkled mysteriously because it was taken out of context. I was in no hurry; I was happy to be in a room that smelled pleasantly of old books, where it was warm and quiet, where the pages rustled as they were turned, as if the books were sighing in their sleep. I was glad I didn't have to go out into the darkness and the snowstorm.

I ran my finger slowly along the undulating spines of the books on the shelf; suddenly my finger disappeared into a dark hollow between a thick French tome on national economy and a book whose torn spine bore the inscription *Geburtshilfe bei Rind und Pferd*. At the rear of the hollow my finger touched an unusually soft and smooth spine. With effort I pulled out from the back of the shelf a book bound in dark-purple velvet that bore neither title nor author's name, and I opened it: the pages were printed in some strange script; I leafed idly through the book. I briefly examined the convoluted arabesques on the fly-leaves and closed the book again. I jammed it back in between the two learned treatises, which had meanwhile drawn breath and filled the gap that remained after the book was removed. I moved further along the shelf but then hesitated and came back, reaching for the book with the purple binding. For a moment I held it aslant, half in, half out of the row of books. Nothing was easier than to put it back level with the rest and continue to browse through other books as I had done on previous occasions, then to go out into the blizzard and continue my walk through the streets before returning home. After all, nothing had happened, nothing to remember, nothing to forget. But I realized that the alphabet in which the book was printed was not of this world. It was still a simple matter to ignore the crevice from which there wafted a disconcerting and alluring breath and allow it to become overgrown with a tissue of renewing circumstances. It was not the first such encounter in my life. Like everyone, I had, on many previous occasions, ignored a half-open door leading elsewhere – in the chilly passages of strange houses, in backyards, on the outskirts of towns. The frontier of our world is not far away; it doesn't run along the horizon or in the depths. It glimmers faintly close by, in the twilight of our nearest surroundings; out of the corner of our eye we can always glimpse another world, without realizing it. We are walking all the time along a shore and along the edge of a virgin forest. Our gestures would seem to rise out of an entity that also encompasses these concealed spaces, and in an odd way they reveal their shadowy existence, although we are unaware of the roar of waves and shrieks of animals – the disquieting accompaniment to our words (and possibly their secret birthplace); we are unaware of the glitter of jewels in the unknown world of nooks and crannies; usually we don't stray off the path even once in the course of our lives. What golden temples in the jungle might we find our way to? With what beasts and monsters might we contend and on what islands might we forget our plans and ambitions? Maybe it was the fascinating flurry of snowy chimeras outside the window or maybe an ironic love of fate, engendered by my failures of recent years, that caused my old fear of crossing frontiers to protest only feebly – as if simply out of habit – and then quickly fall silent; I pulled the book out and opened it once more. I looked at the indifferent letters – rounded but with sharp points at the edges; they were closed or enclosing shapes, convulsed and bristling at one and the same time, but often appearing violently pierced by pointed wedges that penetrated their inner space from outside; elsewhere the bloated letters seemed to be bursting under the pressure of some expanding internal force. I paid for the book at the cash register, put it in my pocket and left the shop. Darkness had fallen outside in the meantime and the snow floundered in the light of the streetlamps.

Back home I switched on the lamp on the desk by the window, then sat down and started to examine the book carefully. I slowly turned the pages, so that one after another they emerged in the ring of lamplight, as if surfacing from the depths of a dark pool; rows of rounded and spiny letters lay on the pages like magic necklaces. In the exhalation of the letters that hovered over the pages there pulsated some kind of somber stories set in jungles and spacious cities; occasionally a scene from one of these stories seemed suddenly to flash before my eyes: the evil face of an intractable disciple of a fantastic heresy, the soft footfall of a wild beast from deep inside a nocturnal palace, an anxious gesture within loose silk, a piece of crumbling stone balustrade among bushes in a garden. I discovered that the book contained several copperplate engravings. The first illustration depicted a broad, deserted square, governed by a sort of dreamlike symmetry with a melancholy sharp perspective of chessboard paving; out of the middle of the square rose an obelisk whose plinth was a regular polygon of smooth stone; on either side of the obelisk stood a three-tiered fountain: on the picture the water falling from one basin to the next gave the impression of a solid, rigid mass. The square was surrounded on its three visible sides by the façades of palaces with monotonous tall colonnades above regular flights of steps. The shadows were short and sharp-cut, suggesting that it was noon on a hot summer day somewhere in the south. At first I thought the square was utterly deserted and only a little while later did I notice a few tiny figures that were out of proportion with the gigantic buildings whose outlines were lost in the thick crosshatching that represented the shadow in the colonnades of the two palaces standing opposite each other. On the marble paving by the wall of the left-hand palace, a young man was lying on his back, his arms outstretched, while a tiger leaned over him holding him down with a mighty paw and tearing at his throat with its teeth. The crudely depicted dark blood spurting from the wound looked like an open fan. By the foot of one of the columns of the palace on the opposite side of the square, several men sprawled at their ease, smoking pipes and playing cards, and were either unaware of what was happening on the other side

4

of the square or unconcerned by it. Between some columns, a short distance away, stood a man and a woman: with a sweep of his arm the man was pointing across the empty space of the sun-drenched square at the murderous tiger, while the woman was wringing her hands, stretching them up towards the lofty caisson vaulting of the colonnade. The second engraving depicted an anatomical section of a pearl-oyster lying on a muddy river bed. The third illustration showed some machine with a complex system of conveyor belts and lots of meshed cogwheels with meticulously hatched teeth.

I left the book open on the desk by the window and went to bed. When I closed my eyes, rows of rounded and spiny letters flashed in front of my eyes, squirming and writhing as they were transformed into snowflakes swirling in the light of the streetlamp. I felt troubled by this alien and unpredictable thing, which I'd introduced into my apartment like a black hen's egg. But I told myself that my anxiety was possibly needless and that the book, like so many disturbing things that have invaded our world, was silently and unobtrusively taking root in an intimately familiar space and soaking up its juices.

I woke up in the middle of the night. When I opened my eyes and stared into the darkness I made out a faint greenish glow shimmering above the open book. I got up and went over to the desk: the letters of the book glimmered; in their faint light, the snowflakes falling on the cornice outside the window glowed green.

# Chapter 2
## In the University Library

I decided to visit the University Library and consult some expert about the book. The researcher they sent me to see inhabited a long, low room beneath the roof, where specks of dust swirled in oblique beams of light, and where crooked and precarious stacks of books were heaped up on tables and the floor. I weaved my way through the piles of books which swayed to the rhythm of my steps. The oval face of a man of some forty years emerged above some books on a writing desk.

When I showed him the book from the second-hand bookshop, he perused it pensively for a long time and then returned it to me, saying: "I'm afraid I can't read these characters and don't even know what nation uses them. But I have come across these letters once before. When I graduated and joined the staff of the University Library I was put in charge of books received from bequests and legacies. One spring, they sent me to look at a large library in an apartment, whose owner had died intestate. They gave me a number on the Smetana Embankment and the name I was to look for on the door. I went there that evening after work. I unlocked the door with the key I'd been given and entered the empty apartment. In the front hall there already wafted towards me the smell of some kind of musty luxury. I walked through the big rooms, which were full of little metal statues of naked women, hounds and horses. Stuffed cushions were strewn everywhere; frills and tassels dangled limply; loosened upholstery covers were rumpled. The walls of one of the rooms was lined from floor to ceiling with glazed bookcases. The dark slope of Petřín Hill with white blossoming trees could be seen in the open window. The sun was just going down alongside the viewing tower; the mauve light of the evening sky spread over the glass of the bookcases. In a bookcase standing by the wall opposite the window there was a dark unglazed recess in which someone had placed an Art Nouveau mirror with an odd, figurative metal base: the oval of the mirror was held in the outstretched hands of a sensuously lolling woman with metal hair streaming behind her. She sat astride the arched back of a dolphin, leaping out of a rigid metal wave. Alongside the mirror a glass flask full of a clear liquid stood on a tripod."

The researcher accompanied his narration with fairly sweeping gestures that riskily agitated the dunes of books on his desk. While he was speaking about the woman on the dolphin he tried to give an approximate rendering of her pose, but in the process the tips of his fingers grazed a column of books: the column teetered, lightly touching the neighboring columns, arousing a torpid swaying motion in them also; luckily, after a while, the researcher managed to calm the waking desk. "Suddenly, behind the glass, in the dying rays of the sun, rubies set into the spine of a leather binding lit up the surrounding gloom. As I touched the glass the sun disappeared behind Petřín Hill and the pale glow of the bookcase was extinguished. I slid the glass door aside in its shallow groove and took out the ruby-studded book. The electricity had been cut off in the apartment, so I went and stood by the open window with the book in order to catch the last light of the day. The book was fastened together with a metal clasp in the shape of a coiled snake with gemstones for eyes. At the very moment I opened the clasp, a bright green light suddenly shone among the trees on the dark hillside of Petřín. A mere coincidence, I told myself, but as soon as I snapped the clasp shut the light immediately went out. I undid the clasp once more and the light reappeared. Its green ray shone in the twilight of the room like a lowered shining lance, and was reflected infinitely in the panes of the bookcases standing opposite each other, creating bewildering frozen rows of sloping green lines, and in the depths of the room it fell onto the center of the oval mirror held by the metallic beauty on her dolphin, where it was reflected and passed right through the middle of the glass flask, which lit up with a poisonous-looking green glow. I had the impression of quiet bubbling coming from the flask, but I was so fascinated by the book held in my hands that I was unconcerned by what was happening in the flask. Yes, I was staring at the very same letters as in the book you've brought. I turned the pages with the strange signs in amazement, and paid no heed to the fact that a sweetish smell was spreading through the room. Shortly, the letters began to undergo a weird transformation. A sort of current pulsated with growing intensity in their lines; the letters lit up and then expired like glowing coals blown with a regular rhythm. Each time they lit up I felt a strange, mounting delight. The pulsation became faster and faster and then everything was quickly extinguished; the letters lay black on the pages of the book like repulsive dead beetles and the sense of delight gave way to a feeling of disgust and horror. I heard the sound of deep roaring. I looked out the window and caught sight of a tsunami wave, about half a mile high, approaching from behind Petřín. It slowly came closer, breaking over the slopes of Petřín, snapping the watchtower in the process. I closed my eyes, waiting to be struck by a terrible torrent. The roaring grew louder and louder, but suddenly fell silent. I stood for a moment with eyes closed, listening to the strange dead silence. Then I opened my eyes and saw a dark wall of water standing outside the window within reaching distance. I leaned out of the window and thrust my fingers into the cool water."

The researcher again demonstrated how he had stretched his arm out of the window and once more set a heap of books in motion; this time the books slithered smoothly off the desk, one after another, some of them in a wide arc, fanning out white pages spectrally in their flight before hitting the floor with a dull thud. The researcher left them lying there and continued his story. "A large black fish stuck its head out of the wall of water and gave a long husky laugh before saying in mocking tones: 'Your whole life you've been trying to forget how you sat alone in the middle of a row of up-tilted seats in a dirty backstreet cinema in Radlice, watching a newsreel with scenes of the sea bed with a shoal of little shiny fish swimming above the fine sand: suddenly the fish clustered together, creating moving statues, depicting you kissing a beautiful artificial girl in the station restaurant at Bakov nad Jizerou (you always found artificial women more attractive; the ticking of their cogs always made you emotional as they lay alongside you in the quiet of the night), a girl who lived

– even though she wrote long letters to her maker saying she was traveling to the Isthmus – in rooming houses with Czech devils, who crunched cookies and nodded when she ingenuously talked to them about pink lamps shining beneath the ice on a pond among nocturnal fields for future recollection on distant dark stars, but were meanwhile secretly planning to dismantle her and assemble from her parts a statue of their Mother, or preferably their very Mother. A cough was heard from the cinema foyer. It was even worse than that gloomy November day when you were walking through the deserted center of a village near Prague and you heard from a loudspeaker attached to a lamp-post a voice ironically reading your study about the Grail of rural post-offices, which lay at the bottom of your desk drawer and which you have never given to anyone to read, because it was your only piece of writing in which you openly named (even with the vilest consonants produced by slovenly and depraved movements of the tongue in the moist darkness of the mouth) the thing that squelches its way out of the deep chasm in the middle of your apartment. Some kind of St Vitus's Cathedral, even bigger than the one at Prague Castle, is moving around the Soběslav district at a speed of 170 mph. The Isthmus rises above the surface of two seas. The piano turned into crabs and crept around the bedroom, the moment was not yet ripe for the music to sound, not yet; the goddesses in silver cases had not yet fallen through the ceiling of the monsters' parliament. The pictogram with the spiral at its center, drawn in pencil on the backs of the lively piano crabs, is pronounced with a sound that resembles a sneeze in a concrete bunker and means forgetting the supple movements of the hand with the green rings in the darkened room in the house above the lake. (There are many and various Chinas on whose outskirts we live; there are rice fields in all the rooms of the adjacent apartment.) You wanted to flee the

10

cinema, but all the doors were locked; when you started to thump on them with your fists, an old usherette shuffled up and told you with forcibly suppressed laughter through the cranny between the doors that you would sit a thousand years in the dark and dirty hall and watch over and over again the most embarrassing scenes of your life enacted on the screen by moving shoals of fish.'

"I don't remember anything else. I was already in the hospital when I awoke. It turned out that there had been a chemical substance in the flask, which, when activated by light of a specific wavelength, released a gas that is a powerful hallucinogenic drug. I was lucky that the neighbors smelt a strange smell and broke into the apartment: they found me lying unconscious on the carpet. The doctors told me that if I'd breathed the gas for much longer, I'd have never awoken from the nightmares and would have gone on living in a Prague under constant threat from tsunami waves arising beyond Petřín Hill and Hradčany, and reviled by black fish. The ruby-encrusted book disappeared from the room and was never found. And until today I have never encountered a book printed in the same script. But I did catch sight of the script on another occasion: it was scratched into the wall of a urinal in a pub at Staré Město pod Landštejnem, alongside a picture of an octopus throttling a tiger with its tentacles."

We both remained silent for a while; he tried with distracted hands to calm the undulations of the books on the desk, but his touch simply disconcerted them all the more and eventually he gave up and sat silently behind the desk gazing out the window at the snow-covered courtyard. "Haven't you tried to investigate the mystery of the book?" I asked him.

"Of course I have. At first I enquired about the book everywhere and drew each of the letters as I recalled them. No one knew anything about the book or the unknown script, but almost everyone would recall some almost forgotten incident or odd encounter that unexpectedly revealed just slightly another space, but usually they would break off in mid-story and quickly change the subject. Someone found a live wriggling starfish on their wet living-room carpet one morning, someone else was waiting for a train one evening at a little station and climbed aboard a car whose interior consisted of a cold Gothic chapel. From the things I heard I started to get the feeling that in our immediate vicinity there lies some strange world. I don't know what it looks like and who lives in it and I don't know what relationship its inhabitants have to us – whether we are indifferent neighbors, whether our delimited space is someone's colony, or whether beyond the walls they are about to wage war. At that period I also started to pay closer attention to the stories told in the staff canteen by the librarians from the lending department, which I hadn't taken very seriously previously; they were horrifying tales of encounters with weird creatures in the unexplored wild reaches of the library. For the first time I let myself be taken to the fringes of those gloomy regions and gazed down passages that led into darkness, telling myself that the very next day I would set off on a journey: I would go to the end of the passage and then keep going. But I kept putting off my departure, telling myself each day: I'll leave it till tomorrow. And eventually I stopped thinking about the mystery of the library, just as I had stopped thinking about the ruby-encrusted book and black fish's malicious laughter. Now I walk around the edges of those dark regions of the library almost every day and I don't even glance into the sinister mouths of those passages and I take no notice of the dismal howls that are heard from their depths. I no longer feel any yearning to cross the frontier. It's too late now to set out on expeditions of exploration."

But I was still full of yearning to learn the mystery of the world from which the book in the purple binding had surfaced, and the researcher's narration simply heightened my impatience. I grabbed him by the sleeve of his dust coat and pleaded with him: "No, it's not too late. On the contrary, it is just the right time. It's a time of defeat and reconciliation with fate that gives rise to determination, and the snow lying everywhere is almost already the beginning of the unreal. It too urges us to leave: we are bound to find in it footprints of chimerical beings, footsteps that will lead us to secret lairs in the depths of the city. Leave everything behind and come with me, we'll set out on an expedition together. We'll find rare gems and splendid monsters, you'll see. Most important of all, my guess is that beyond the frontiers is hidden the secret of our world. We'll only be able to live for real when we return from the other side. Even before, I often used to have the feeling that the floor plan of the customs that create our world is like the ornament on the mosaic floor at Knossos, whose frozen lines are said to have preserved the path of the movements of ritual dancers – masked figures who disappeared long ago: there is hope that beyond the frontier we will finally glimpse the primordial dance of which our world is a trace."

"No, I don't think there is any point in leaving," he said softly. "I'm not enticed anymore either by gems or monsters. Maybe the source of our world's shapes is really hidden beyond the frontier, but we would never be able to understand it anyway; it could have no meaning for us. The only thing that is meaningful and understandable for us is what moves along the paths of our world, what follows the lines of our ornament in Knossos, wherever its origins lie, whether they are the trace of the dances of exalted gods, or the record of the capers of a drunken demon. We wouldn't be able to talk about a primordial dance because speech is inadequate to describe what was here before the emergence of ornament. We wouldn't even be able to see the primordial dance because vision is so embedded in the mesh of familiar sense, that whatever is not nourished by that sense would remain invisible to us."

"But what about the starfish on the carpet, the Gothic-chapel railroad car and the books with the mysterious script?" I objected. "After all, people from our world encountered them."

"Those are just things that happen to get washed up on our shore, which we have enveloped in some compensatory meaning on the basis of false similarities with our own experience. The anxious and cunning deity of grammar holds its protective hand over us, and conceals the monsters' faces; we say 'that thing's a mystery' and 'that incident is uncanny,' but in doing so we discreetly wrap their dreadful presence, their sinister essence, unrelated to anything and defying our gaze, in metaphor, as if in an old threadbare suit and so assign them a place in our world. It can't be helped. It doesn't matter who drew the pattern on our mosaic floor, it still remains our prison and our home. It is quite likely to be the trace of some repulsive and dreadful dance by some mad god, but if we were able to find out about it somehow, we would have to accept that madness: the only thing that would be truthful and meaningful for us would still only be what was coherent in the world of that madness. Don't concern yourself with weird books that remind you of the frontiers of our world. They can't lead you out of it, they can only eat away at its structure from within. The frontier of our world is a line with only one side. There is no path from the inside out, nor can there be."

14

# Chapter 3
## Petřín

There was probably a lot of truth in what the researcher at the Clementinum said about the frontier, but I could not agree with him on every point. I had this recurring hunch that we also at some time had had a share in that primordial dance, that we too had taken part in the revelry, that we ourselves had been that dancing deity or demon, and that we have retained traces of old memories and a dim sympathy for what we subsequently renounced and shunted off over the frontier. I didn't lose the yearning to discover the world from which the book with the unknown script had come. That very afternoon I set off for snow-covered Petřín hoping to find a clue to the mysterious green light. I slithered down icy paths, falling and straying among trees whose branches sprinkled snow on me as I struggled through snow-drifts. I gazed into the depths of the shrubbery. I looked through broken windows and holes in closed shutters into the dark interiors of the cottages and locked summerhouses that stood in the hillside, but all I could see were abandoned garden implements, cans of paint and torn paper sacks, from which some light-colored powder had trickled. Towards evening I gave up; I was just about to make my way down to the path that would take me to the streetcar stop at Újezd, when, in a shallow hollow between snowy trees, I caught sight of an upright cylinder, waist-high, whose lid was covered in a thick layer of snow. A memory suddenly came back: when we used to play hide-and-seek on Petřín as children, I had hidden on several occasions behind this very cylinder; it had been summer then and the cylinder was overgrown with long grass. I recalled how I had always tried to open a little rusty iron window in the upper part of the cylinder that resembled a stove door, but I had never managed to. I expect it is some container for sand or cinders, I thought to myself. Amazingly, on this occasion the little window immediately gave way when I pressed the catch and it opened with a long drawn-out screech. I leaned over and thrust my head inside.

When my eyes became used to the dark, I discovered that the cylinder was actually the skylight turret of a cupola, which widened out beneath it, overarching the nave of a church, the floor of which was lost in the dark depths. The nave was encircled by twelve chapels, in the middle of each of which there stood a large glass statue. The statues were hollow and filled with water; swimming in the water were various sea creatures, some of which were dimly phosphorescent: their pale light, the sole illumination inside the church, was reflected in restless glimmers on the countless folds of golden ornaments in the style of a kind of gloomy subterranean Baroque, which meandered over the walls and on the broad frames of dark paintings. It occurred to me that the statues formed a complete series, a serial in glass, depicting in chronological order scenes from the life of some hero or god. They represented some kind of cruel conflicts, lonely ecstasy and painful annunciation. Unrest and struggle prevailed inside the statues too, as the sea creatures ceaselessly pursued and snapped at each other with sharp teeth. I watched a horrified glowing fish seek refuge in the head of a statue when a swiftly moving dark shadow suddenly appeared from behind. At that moment the glass face, screwed up in an unknown spasm, lit up in the darkness of the church as if in some sudden mystical rapture; a moment later, however, the agile predator caught up with the little fish and sank its teeth into it; the light was extinguished within the dark blood that gradually spread and soon filled the entire head of the sculpture. Behind the altar stood a thirteenth sculptural group of glass; it depicted a scene already familiar to me: a tiger devouring a prostrate young man. Inside the body of the tiger a solitary jellyfish slowly undulated with a roseate glow.

Suddenly lights came on at the ends of the interlacing branches of a chandelier hanging from a long cable attached to the turret of the cupola right next to my head; the light of the fish in the statues paled in the glare of the chandelier, but most of the space within the church remained in semi-darkness. People were entering the church (apparently via some underground passage) and sitting in the pews. A priest appeared behind the altar; he was a swarthy, fifty-year-old man with slicked-down black hair and a narrow moustache; a green and purple vestment with gold embroidery hung from him in heavy, rigid folds. He stood in silent concentration for a moment, with head bowed, before commencing his sermon.

"Today we recall the fifteenth day of the Exile's peregrination, when, in the dark of evening, his bark completed its journey along the stream to the city. The stinking torrent was lined by houses, factories and ramshackle palaces with high walls of bare brick from which iron girders protruded over the stream, as well as the mouths of wide pipes from which dirty water flowed. Crumbling steps ran down to the river from the backyards of the houses, with moldering objects and brownish foam clinging to them. Above the backyards, dark verandahs were attached to the walls and the lights of kitchens could be seen. *The Book of Deserted Gardens* speaks of this on the page with the greasy stain from noodle soup left by a scribe of long ago, who took fright when across the sun-drenched page there fell the horned shadow of a monster as it passed through the sleepy and desolate lanes of the city after defeating the aging king at a game of chess on the parched ramparts. It was played with chessmen of sparkling ice; all that could be heard in the silence was the soft rattle of red and purple gemstones falling in the hour-glass alongside the chessboard; it was the monster's vengeance for a bygone defeat in a contest beneath the high stone wall of the fortress, on which broke the waves of the nocturnal sea. The stories do not tell the entire truth – monsters always return: one day, a familiar monster will ring your doorbell too, bearing a chessboard under its arm; it will persuade you to join it in a game of chess and you will be obliged to include in the game the carved figure of a tiger-headed spearman, a piece that moves in irregular, furtive spirals and can stray quite far from the chessboard – even out of the apartment. Monsters return and their claws sink into even our most intimate velvets and scratch a drawing into the mirror in the lobby depicting the woman you love best of all proudly engaged in a silent and dark orgy with six obese men aboard a subterranean bomber, boring deep down through earth and stone and then surfacing – its black nose like the snout of an enormous vole – out of the paving on National Avenue in front of windows of the Sla-

18

via Café, at the very moment when the young poet, seated there over a cup of coffee, finally decides to leave unfinished his poem about the shining rulers of the cities of Inner Asia, because he has grown weary of writing on a typewriter, whose type bars refuse to fall on the paper in orderly fashion, but every so often bend at their joints, stretch out and slash his face with the poison thorns at their tips, so that after the hundred and twentieth hexameter, his head, which women admired and stroked just one month earlier, has swollen into a ball, beneath whose taut and increasingly transparent skin is permeated by the green pus of sores. Why doesn't he choose another typewriter? All the other typewriters have disappeared: some have been borne away to the Caucasus by a swarm of locusts (it is proven that, by joining forces, locusts are capable of carrying even a horse many miles), some typewriters are used as part of some kind of new perversion spreading through the cities, and some have been transformed into the white light illuminating the statue of the beautiful animal angel. The Exile in his little boat reflected lengthily on why the large brick-built palaces in the city through which he was traveling bore such a resemblance to railroad stations, and for the first time ever in his life he was tempted to leave the sacred books on the cypress islands at the mercy of the monotonous comments of the goblins, who were gradually filling up all the margins and already beginning to write over the text itself, as well as at the mercy of dubious commentaries, which talked over and over again about the sadness of the empty and locked dance halls of village inns, where the chair legs stick up toward the ceiling with its damp patches, dance halls that will apparently play an important role in post-mortal tourism. There awoke within him a temptation to leave everything behind and become the demon of the dirty city river, to thrust his head out of the dark waters every evening and gaze at the lights of the kitchen windows, to live off the food that housewives would put out for him in dishes on the last step above the river's surface, to forget about the white marble of the broad squares, glowing into the night and coldly flowing into the day, beautiful as the incurable despair on quiet summer afternoons in big rooms with windows giving onto gardens. In the end it was a piece of rotten wood floating on the surface that helped him overcome the temptation: he recognized in it a fragment of the small domestic altar before which she, who canoodled in the corridor of the sleeping car with the cruel Minotaur of the trains, first removed her headband and showed him her old scar, which remained from the wound inflicted on her with its steel beak by a bird that was lost in the mirrors, when she leaned her forehead against the cool glass to calm a fever that started to burn in her when she first caught sight of a flamingo pursuing a devil on the long empty corridor of offices covered in shiny linoleum: the only things that continue to penetrate our space are the sharp metal beaks of evil birds and the three-foot-long stingers of giant wasps that sting our faces when we are shaving; the dull buzzing of wasps behind the glass of the mirror can be heard when we're reading a book on the couch in the evening; sometimes it starts to form itself into words, and then we hear a voice reminiscent of the old revelation that we betrayed; it was the revelation we received from the sphinx that we caught sight of when we were eighteen on one of our solitary walks, lying on a flaking metal bed frame that stood in the middle of a field above Chuchle; darkness was falling, and beyond the twilit snow-covered plain the lights of a car slid along the road to Slivenec: in the end we forgot the revelation that penetrated us on that snowy field like a red-hot sword point; we are reminded of it from time to time only by the voice that emerges from the dull buzzing of the giant wasps returning tirelessly annoyed at dusk from the other side of the mirror. What will happen when they finally break through the glass? At that moment it will be necessary to spit the diamonds from our mouth and try to find the fire we once hid in our bookcase. Pain enables the creation of new species of transparent creatures, lamps shine in honey, and in the dark and cold railroad waiting-room cries can still be heard, even though the man and woman from whose mouths they were once emitted here, now lie in white Hindustan on a mosaic floor and with trembling hands tenderly caress each other's bodies, covered in a shiny mottled fur. When the Exile caught sight of the fragment of the familiar altar on the surface, he recalled the leopards on the white staircases of his native palace and he determined to submerge himself in the warm and sticky filth of home that adheres to us throughout our lives and that we wash off in glittering hotels throughout our lives. There are commentators who maintain that he should have yielded to the temptation, that he should have become the demon of the filthy river and every evening sung beneath the open kitchen windows the song of the centaurs' unending battles with the machine. In all events what decision he made was utterly immaterial: that is the chief message of today's sermon that you should meditate on this week."

A monotonous tinkling could be heard; maybe it was supposed to be music. The priest spread his arms and the gold emblems embroidered on his vestment flattened out to reveal depictions of tigers. He raised his voice: "We too must one day decide between cold marble and the sad songs heard from a can with a cod painted on its label. And our decision also, however superhuman, will be immaterial; whether we choose one or the other, we will end up walking along an endless concrete plain wearing a metal dog mask . . ."

The worshippers in their pews opened their hymn books and started to sing a long drawn-out wordless melody in which I could detect no rhythm or system, and which most resembled the random sounds of wind shaking tin window seals on winter evenings. I listened to the strange song and waited to see if anything else would happen, but there was simply the sound of that formless singing, just unending intonements of a single note, after which the melody would abruptly rise or fall and remain fixed once more into a long single note. The singing was putting me to sleep and I was starting to feel cold, so I removed my head from the cylinder: it was already dark and the city lights twinkled below me through the black branches. The funicular, its lights switched on, was silently ascending the slope. I ran down to Újezd through the deep snow and boarded a streetcar arriving from Malá Strana Square. The car was almost empty; I gazed at the pale image of the streetcar's illuminated interior reflected in the dark windows and pondered on the underground church. I still did not know whom I had actually encountered on Petřín. Had I come upon some secret sect? Had I witnessed the birth of a new faith? Maybe it would extend from beneath Petřín and dominate the world. Or, on the contrary, was the underground worship the dying tremor of an ancient religion? Were the visitors to the temple foreigners who had assembled in Prague for some reason to celebrate their religious holiday, or have they been living for centuries alongside us unobserved? Or had I found myself on the frontier of an unknown city adjoining our own? Is it a city growing out of the waste that our own order has not been able to consume and throw away, or is it a community of autochthons, who were here before we arrived and to whom we are of so little account that they will not even notice when we depart? What is the ground plan of that city? What districts is it divided into and what are its laws? Where are its boulevards, squares and gardens, where its gleaming royal palace?

# Chapter 4
## The Malá Strana Café

I made several more expeditions to Petřín, but once again the little window in the turret of the church was always stuck. I would shake it with all my might but never managed to open it. I carried the purple book with me all the time; I would open it in the streetcar, when standing in line in a shop, and sometimes while walking along the street, and I would examine the strange signs over and over again. By now I could recognize the individual letters, even though I did not know the sounds they represented: I was struck by the fact that there were seventy-six signs. Either the script distinguished between sounds that we regard as variations on a single phoneme, or it represented an abundance of sounds that are completely different from our phonemes. I tried to imagine these sounds; sometimes I would try pronouncing them aloud as I walked along, and passersby would turn and gaze at me in astonishment. At the same time I realized that the small number of phonemes that we use are hemmed in by an unknown primeval forest of sounds: and since the meanings of words grow mysteriously out of phonic matter, that virgin forest is full of disquieting seeds of phantasmal things, beings and events. Why did the users of the strange script feel such a need to differentiate the sounds graphically? Was it their enjoyment of the richness of meaning of the sound that prompted them to make the text resemble a musical score, which would capture the life forces pulsating within the language, or, on the contrary, was the overabundance of letters a sign of angst that meanings that are too closely tied to a single shade of sound constantly escape? The tension that exuded from the shapes of the letters tended to suggest that they grew out of a world of anxiety. The great number of letters could be evidence of a tendency to pedantic descriptiveness, I said to myself, but also of a desperate yearning to come closer to the dark primeval cry, which, in speech, reaches out into the future in an effort to be overheard by some approaching deity. I also wondered about the meaning of the little convoluted signs suspended above some of the letters: did they indicate the length or accent, the melody, or the gesture or grimace that should accompany the sound when pronounced? But maybe those inconspicuous little pothooks and loops were what conveyed the main burden of the text and the big letters were simply ornamentation or a confusing message intended to mislead strangers? Or perhaps those tiny signs were the remnants of an old hieratic language, which remained on the fringes of the message like the ruins of palaces of extinct empires on the outskirts of new towns – remnants that are now understood only by a sect of devotees, who read only this tiny and neglected text in the books and are maybe waiting until the old gods return and these signs will once again grow and glitter above the façades of revived temples.

I realized that what aroused the greatest apprehension and disquiet was not the fossilized existence of signs without meaning, but rather the astonishing experience that nothing can be entirely divested of the emanation of meaning, or rather the presence of a strange significance, which quivered over the letters like St Elmo's Fire, a significance that was not so much some odd peculiarity of the rest of the script as a meaning that pervades everything that is, and which, on the pages of the book in the purple binding became suddenly visible, because it was not hidden as it tends to be otherwise. Are they significances that we are accustomed to, and which would seem to derive their mystery from that primordial message of being, as from a spring, and they renew their life within it, while at the same time it corrodes them and they die of it, as of some latent illness? Was I justified in saying I didn't understand the book at all? Out of the tangle of anxieties that were aroused when I looked at the pages of the book covered in the alien letters, the strongest and strangest anxiety of all stemmed from the suspicion that there was nothing to understand or seek answers to, anxiety from the feeling that some dreadful victory constantly lurks in wait for us, and we dread it more than the greatest defeat.

I sat in the half-empty Malá Strana Café by a window with a view of the snow-covered square, the book open in front of me. The cold afternoon light glistened on the gray marble of the table. A new customer came in: a thin, elderly man with an agitated expression and jerky movements, one of those lonely individuals that surface during the afternoon in the cafés of Malá Strana. As he passed me he noticed the open book; he started, uncertain for a moment whether to keep going. But then, taking a cautious look round the room, he suddenly leaned towards me and asked where I had obtained the book. I explained how I had come by it. He sat down on the edge of the empty chair opposite me, like a puppet whose strings had been released too quickly by its operator, and at the selfsame moment he leaned right across the table, and, while continuing to look around him restlessly, said to me in a low, pleading whisper: "Take my advice and get rid of that book right away. Believe me when I tell you that ever since I came upon those accursed letters, I have wandered the dismal world of the outskirts like a befuddled dog and have no peace. Just look at the artful and crafty expression in those letters! It's an evil gangrene that will gradually overwhelm everything. The letters exhale a poison that discreetly and assiduously corrodes the familiar things of our world. You'll see: in its breath the shapes of our buildings disintegrate into the outlines of barbarian temples shining with a repulsive magnificence; a forgotten evil gold will start to glitter. The poison corrodes our words and transforms them into the old anxiety-ridden sounds of the primeval forest, into the lonely music of the statues. Life will turn into a scarcely intelligible role in an unending performance of an obscene myth about a young god dying in the jungle."

While he was speaking, he kept sliding closer to me on his elbows across the tabletop, and ended up almost lying on it. I asked him to tell me where he had come across the mysterious writing. He relaxed slightly and slid back a short distance.

"The dreadful story started in the sixties. At that time I was teaching at the law faculty. I had first started publishing articles in specialized journals when I was still a student and everyone predicted a great career for me. I had a nice wife and two little children. I had never made any overtures to any of my female students, but some time in the mid-sixties a woman student suddenly appeared in the first year, whose face painfully attracted me for some unknown reason. Her gestures seemed to me to have grown out of some strange, mysterious space and were still rooted there."

"What space was it?" I asked him, because spaces growing out of gestures interested me.

"They were large empty halls clad with marble. We are always attracted to women by spaces that have been absorbed into their bodies, landscapes with which they have been saturated and which shine from their movements when we meet them. If only I'd known what dark empire was beckoning me in the quiet undulation of beloved hands . . . I had the impression she enjoyed my company. We bumped into each other one day in the Old Town and I invited her to a glass of wine. Then I accompanied her home. We walked down some dark steps toward her apartment. She lived in Neruda Street, in one of those houses that is built into the hillside and is always a surprise for visitors, who, after climbing a narrow staircase up to the top floor, then leave from there by a back door onto solid ground. I became a regular visitor to her flat. I was amazed to find she lived alone in an apartment with several large rooms, but she never told me anything about herself. We didn't speak much at all. We would lie in the darkened room and listen to voices from the street. We would look at the statues on the façade of the palace opposite, which could be seen from the window. The girl's touch once more spoke of a strange land, with its grass and leaves and the paws of its animals . . ."

He faltered and again looked uneasily around the room, but there were only a few pensioners and students sitting in the café and no one paid us any attention. Even so, he crept a little closer across the table and spoke even more softly. "In the hallway I would pass a white-painted door that was always locked. Above it someone had inscribed several strange letters into the door frame. The door was on the side of the building facing the hillside . . . It had a mysterious fascination for me, but my girlfriend told me that it was just the door to a utility room with old junk. Once, when she ran downstairs to go to the store, I couldn't resist it. I took a bunch of keys down from a hook in the wall and tried to see if any of them would turn the lock in the white door. After several attempts one of the keys turned in the lock . . ."

At that instant we both noticed a waiter in a tight vest scurrying over to our table, waving with one hand at the man sitting opposite me while miming with the other that the man was wanted on the telephone. "Nobody knows I'm here," the man said apprehensively, but he got up and went off to the cloakroom. I waited impatiently for him to return and finish his story. Meanwhile I looked out of the window as large flakes of wet snow slowly fell to the ground. I watched a green streetcar emerge from the bend of Letná Street, its roof covered in a thick layer of snow. It silently came to a halt outside the café window. It was the same shape as regular Prague streetcars, but its body seemed to be carved out of a single piece of marble; its windows were of dark opaque glass. The front door of the streetcar opened and out dashed two men with long curly beards and wearing heavy, gray ankle-length coats. They were carrying a stretcher. They ran with long, coordinated, ballet-like leaps, and they stuck out their chests. They disappeared through the door of the café, but a moment later they emerged once more, still loping with the same regular strides, but this time there was a lifeless figure lying on the stretcher. I did not need to look to see who it was. It is sufficient to open a forbidden door out of curiosity once, I thought to myself, and what creeps out of it will follow you into cafés, shove you into a stretcher and run with you through a snowy square from the nineteen sixties until now. The stretcher-bearers dashed into the streetcar and the door immediately closed behind them. The streetcar moved off and a moment later had disappeared.

I rushed outside, leaped into one of the cabs that was waiting for customers in the car park outside the café, and requested the apathetic and sleepy cab driver to follow the green streetcar. The snow was falling even harder now and it struck the windshield in wads. Through gaps in the snow, repeatedly renewed by the rapidly oscillating wipers, the back of the mysterious streetcar came nearer and then receded again. At first the streetcar ran along the regular tracks, but when we reached the suburbs it suddenly turned off onto a steep deserted street where no streetcars ever went. It slowly passed long factory walls and then the walls of tired houses decorated with dreamy women's faces of chipped stucco. Old junk covered in plastic sheets was piled up on little balconies with blackened pillars. I recalled how, in the course of my long walks on the city's outskirts, I occasionally noticed streetcar tracks set absurdly into the asphalt of out-of-the-way streets. I had never given it any thought. I had simply assumed them to be some old factory tracks that were now disused and no one had bothered to remove.

Eventually the streetcar passed through a residential area of family homes on a hilltop, past cottages with flaking façades set deep within snowy gardens, where water pumps wrapped in old rags bound with twine stood alongside frozen water barrels. It had stopped snowing and in the west there was a break in the clouds, and pale evening sunlight was filtering down the walls and tree trunks. The cottages and gardens suddenly ended; the road wound its way round the last fences and beyond it was a snowy plain sloping up to a dark wood toward which the red sun was now descending, its rays coloring pink the untrodden snow of the plain. At the end of the street that led to the plain stood a ramshackle single-story house; above the street entrance a scarcely legible sign on the wall read Tavern. The blind side wall of the tavern faced the snow-covered field. The streetcar passed the tavern and entered the plain with its untrodden pink covering of snow. The snow spattered up on either side like when a boat is launched into the water; reddish light shone through the geyser of snow. Slowly the streetcar disappeared in the direction of the wood, leaving behind it a deep curved furrow, accentuated by a dark shadow, like a sweeping charcoal stroke on pink paper. I thrust money into the cab driver's hand and leaped out of the car. I ran after the streetcar but sank knee-deep into the snow. There was no hope of my catching up with the streetcar. I stopped and watched the streetcar moving behind the dark wood; then all that could be seen was the pink snow and the motionless trees, whose jagged shadows stretched down the plain toward me. I turned and went back across the snow-covered field in the direction of the city, toward the cottages, in whose windows there glistened the last rays of the sun. A bus passed along the road, coming from a village over the horizon. A dog's bark could be heard from the gardens.

# Chapter 5
# The Gardens

Before I reached the city limits the light had gone from the windows of the cottages and the snow had darkened. The tavern was already lit up and the lamp above the entrance shone on the dirty trampled snow on the low front steps. I went inside to have a drink to wash down my unsuccessful pursuit of the mysterious streetcar. I found myself in a large, overheated room. In the middle of it stood a billiard table, the green baize sharply lit by a low-hanging bare bulb. The corners of the room could not be seen through the gloom and cigarette smoke. Men in unbuttoned flannel shirts sat squashed around Formica-topped tables, pushed together in twos or threes. The men's faces gleamed with sweat. Above them on the walls hung posters of football teams and naked women posing under a waterfall. From a dark alcove the half-open door of a coal stove glowed orange. In the bluish square of the tavern window were spread the twisted branches of trees in the back garden, which was sinking into the approaching night. I squeezed into a space in the middle of a long bench by the wall. I turned my head sideways and buried it wearily in the heavy bunches of coats hanging on the wall behind me; the humidity of the melting snow awoke heady and unidentifiable odors within them. I listened to the pleasant murmur of the tavern in which the voices of the customers were blended. Little glasses of green liqueur shone from the gloomy corners of the room like lost gemstones.

On one side I was pressed against a thick-set man with a round, red face, who spoke to no one but slowly sipped his beer while reading *Our Garden* magazine. When I finished my second glass of beer I turned to him and asked him whether he knew anything about the mysterious green marble streetcar. He said nothing and did not even stir; I thought he had not even heard my question, but when I had ceased to expect an answer and had returned my attention to my beer, he suddenly said, as his gaze wandered in the gloom of the other side of the room: "It appears in our part of town at night, in fog or during snowstorms. The people that go aboard it are never seen again. In one passageway I saw an inscription scratched into the plaster that said the green streetcar's depot is in the courtyard of a monastery in Tibet, and that it arrives here via secret routes across forests and fields. There could be something in it. A man at the barber's was saying how he was picking mushrooms in the forest one summer when all of a sudden the streetcar silently passed by him and then disappeared into the mist. But others maintain that it's a streetcar from the depths of the Atlantic Ocean, which, from time to time, for some unknown reason, heads for the mouths of rivers and then runs upstream along the riverbed, surfacing at evening and then wandering around the country, past old factories on the outskirts and along the wooden fences of football pitches until it reaches the city. There are rumors that under the plaster in some rotunda restorers uncovered a Romanesque fresco, on which something strikingly similar to a green streetcar can be seen in the background behind Prince Břetislav . . ."

A tipsy young man in sweatpants came over to our table and started to bargain over the price of a bag of cement with the man who had told me about the streetcar. He then turned to me and tried to find out whether we knew each other from the Sparta football ground; when he saw I wasn't in the mood for conversation, he made a dismissive gesture with his hand and sat down at the next table.

"The tracks run through gardens, shrubberies and fences," my neighbor suddenly said once more. "We'll be lying in bed at night when we hear the clanging coming closer from the depths of the gardens. Lights sweep across the ceiling and the pattern of the curtains is projected huge onto the wall in the dazzling light. Our wives grab our hands in dread. But during the day we avoid mentioning the streetcar. The streetcar always stands between us like a dark shadow. We are afraid of our children asking us about it . . ." He fell silent and drank his beer. I sensed that he was hesitating over whether to continue his narration. And then he spoke, after all: "When our daughter was growing up I used to say to my wife: you'll have to take her to one side and tell her all about the green streetcar. She is inexperienced and could easily come to harm. My wife spoke to our daughter several times, telling her to be cautious and beware of the streetcar, but our daughter just scoffed and said there was nothing to fear, that she wasn't the sort of person who'd get on any old streetcar, particularly if it was green. But when we were coming home from her first ball we were waiting at night at an unlit streetcar stop . . ." Again he fell silent and I urged him to continue, because I had an idea what was going to happen. "Suddenly a streetcar pulled up. It moved so quietly we didn't even notice it coming. Our daughter, who was tired and had her head full of memories of the ball, stepped through the door when it opened directly opposite her . . . When she was inside I realized that the streetcar was a strange color. I shouted out and hurled myself at the streetcar to drag her back, but the door closed in a flash and my hands struck cold opaque glass. The streetcar moved off and disappeared into the darkness . . ."

We both fell silent. The murmur of voices in the tavern rose and fell like the surf of a mysterious sea. "That was almost twenty years ago," he said quietly. "We've never met our daughter since, except for a few occasions when we've caught sight of her face in the depth of a mirror in a darkened room, and sometimes we've caught the sound of her voice in the roaring of a stove. At first we would occasionally come across slips of paper at the bottom of drawers or between the pages of books, bearing sad messages that we would understand less and less: she would write about halls through which there flowed rivers with rafts carrying bronze lions, and also about never-ending symposia in fossilized forests, or about cafés, where the waiter would emerge out of thick mist. From what she wrote us it would seem that she is living in some kind of world where folds in fabric are more important than faces and have names, whereas thickets of faces merge into an indifferent blur. Also words there would seem to be regarded as an insignificant accompaniment to humming and rustling, which alone carry important messages. Sometimes the lines of writing in her letters became unraveled and undulated all over the paper before becoming knotted again into meaningless tangles, from which emerged the beginnings of disturbing words and pictures. Her world is difficult for us to understand. What I long for most of all in the world is to see her once again, but I am not sure whether we would understand each other any more if we did meet. Often it occurs to me that the world she lives in might be close by, because its solidities are located where in our world we see only space, and its space is solidity in our world . . ."

He stopped speaking. For a while he stared at the poster-covered wall opposite, and then he lowered his head and continued reading *Our Garden*. We went on sitting side by side for a long while and both drank several more beers, but neither of us uttered another word. Eventually his neighbor across the table persuaded him to play a game of cards and I paid my check and got dressed. I walked down a cold passage, between walls painted with a pattern that resembled Chinese faces, to a cramped toilet. The light inside was not working; the dark snow-covered garden was visible through the open window. I thought I could hear drawn-out singing coming from its depths, just like I'd heard from the underground temple. I went to the end of the passage and opened the door that led into the garden; I sank deep into snow that had drifted against the wall of the building. The frost crept through my sleeves and pant legs like a nocturnal snake onto my bare skin. When I closed the door behind me, the voices from the tavern fell silent. I was standing on the edge of dark snow-covered gardens; twisted trees were turning black against the snow, the light from distant lamps glittering through their branches like gleaming fruit. From within the gardens came the sound of a magical music to which I felt irresistibly drawn. I walked through the untrodden snow in the direction of its notes into the dark depths of the garden. Beyond a ruined face there was another garden. I walked drunkenly through the snowy gardens, between bare trees from which wrinkled apples hung here and there, past compost heaps, crooked sheds, empty rabbit hutches, and one fence after another. Maybe the streetcar would suddenly emerge from between the trees. Maybe, in the bushes, the diamonds on the tiara of the Queen of the Gardens would suddenly glisten. But nothing moved anywhere except for the branches waving in the wind. All that could be heard in the silence, apart from the monotonous music, was the occasional distant bark of a dog. I came upon a rotting gazebo and discovered that what I had taken for liturgical singing was simply nocturnal music produced by a piece of tin on its roof as it quivered in the wind. I sat down in the gazebo, through whose large empty windows could be seen the black trees, the snow, and the distant lights. There was the sound of soporific music, as meaningless as the drawings made by the tangle of branches on the canvas of blue snow, like the damp stains on the walls that I stagger by alone, like the strange contorted letters in evil books. Where am I bound, for God's sake? Why don't I turn back to the other people while there is still time? But the thing that wafted from those nocturnal gardens and from the fringes of our space already had me in its power.

I walked onward. I climbed through several more holes in fences and then at the end of a garden I caught sight of streetlights. I scrambled up onto some decoratively incised palings and jumped down onto the sidewalk. In a short while I had reached a bus stop. I waited for a bus and whiled away the time by reading in the faint purplish light of the fluorescent lamp some cards pinned to the back of a glass-fronted box that someone had attached with wire to the garden fence; it was a display-case such as are generally used for the notices of gardeners' associations or hiking clubs. The cards consisted of various advertisements and notices: someone offered strawberry seedlings, someone else had for sale a couch and a wedding dress displayed on a crumpled photograph of a bride with her head cut off. In the bottom corner, between a piece of paper on which someone announced that they repaired refrigerators and a cyclostyled notice about compulsory dog vaccinations, there was a card on which someone had typed: "A lecture on the subject of Latest Discoveries about the Great Battle in the Bedrooms will take place on Wednesday at 2:30 A.M. in the Arts Faculty." I heard the approaching bus. The doors opened with a hiss and I climbed aboard.

# Chapter 6
# The Nocturnal Lecture

Wednesday was the following day: although there was no date given on the card, I was so impatient to discover something new about the world whose contours had been revealed to me, that I decided to take a look at the Arts Faculty that very night. I came there via the Old Town Square. The fluorescent lamps buzzed into the silence of the empty, snow-covered street. The massive Arts Faculty building loomed darkly at the end of a row of houses. When I reached it, I stood and looked upward, but I could see no lighted window, only the light of the fluorescent streetlamps reflected in the first-floor windowpanes. The main entrance in the colonnade was unlocked and I went in. It was dark and cold in the empty building. I walked past the deserted, glazed-in reception and went up the wide staircase. I walked around the corridor with windows onto the courtyard. Now and then I stopped and listened, but the building was as silent as the grave. All I could hear was the sound of night streetcars rattling along the embankment. I opened the doors of lecture rooms and looked in, but they were all dark and empty. Only when I opened the door of one of the third-floor lecture rooms did I see people in overcoats seated at benches behind desks in the cold room, faintly lit by the fluorescent light, while the monotonous voice of the lecturer could be heard from the lectern. A beam of feeble light fell on his gaunt face with its pointed goatee beard. I sat down at an empty space on the edge of a bench by the door.

I heard: "Until just a few years ago the scientific community, with the rare exception, was of the view that the great battle in the depths of bedrooms could not be regarded as a historic event. It was maintained that the records in the reference books were not reliable and were the result of the historicization of certain rituals connected with underground celebrations of expulsion of dragons from savings banks. It was also constantly pointed out that there was no reference to the battle in the famed Lion's Chronicle, which was found, as you all know, on a rainy night in a plastic wrapper on a seat in an unlit compartment, just as the train stopped on the track and the compartment was just beneath the lighted window of an Art Nouveau villa at Všenory, the light of which was reflected in the wet leaves of the darkened garden. It is truly astonishing that the scholars who were hypercritical about the source materials should not have found it odd that the chronicle was found precisely outside a villa in whose window could be seen dimly on the wall part of a picture on which could be discerned the figures of fauns dancing in a meadow. It would seem that none of the historians noticed that the small object painted in the grass below the birch tree bore a striking resemblance to the scrubbing brush still used in the spa-temple, where, one evening, the priest said into the clouds of steam rolling over the baths: 'In the buffet in a distant town, on a blackboard with the names and prices of the meals, is written in chalk the last message of the Lord of the Outskirts – a warning that the blackened interiors of vases exhale into our space. This breath, declares the Lord of the Outskirts, corrodes the old constellations. Nor must you forget the impatient and nimble pincers of machines lurking behind long walls in the streets of Smíchov. Nirvana will not take the place of a promenade concert.' It is irrelevant that the colored shape's resemblance to a scrubbing brush turned out to be fortuitous (it actually turned out to be a depiction of a mushroom or a blob of latex). And let's remember something else too: the letter F at the beginning of the word faun in the alphabet of our neighbors is shaped like an upright rod with two crossbars running horizontally from it at the middle and the top, in other words, exactly like that structure on the edge of the city, from which, every evening – standing on the bottom rung and resting his telescope on the top one – the restless false mayor used to watch out for a procession of women, which had to try to take silver wolves with ruby eyes into the city and deploy them behind long curtains in bedrooms. But all he saw that time were the distant lights of automobiles on the freeway, like a cold, shiny necklace. Is this truly all mere coincidence? The situation changed radically when a new generation of historians took over, unburdened by positivist prejudices. The latest research, particularly the most recent discoveries in the field of the archeology of drawers, proves unequivocally not only that the battle really took place, but also, apparently, that it continues. The golden monuments to its heroes flash from the depths of the mirror in a dark corner of the bedroom whenever the slowly revolving light of the lighthouse falls on it. When the residents of the apartments go to the bathroom at night via the dark front hall, their foot sometimes lands on a swaying pontoon: there are few who dare to walk along the rickety pontoon bridge into the darkness, although many know that at its end they would be allowed to forget their names and touch with their foreheads the cool metal of pipes carrying the milk of distressed animals to the chimerical cities on the coast. At night they catch sight of a figure in camouflage dress with a Persian-rug pattern dashing through the bedroom. They find field-telephone wires beneath the bed. A trench runs across a dark corner of the room. During dinner, lurking eyes glitter above it. A child is wont to say: 'There's something in the corner, I'm going to take a look,' but its parents quickly call it to order: 'No leaving the table during the meal!' They are all afraid to take notice of the war being waged in the nooks and crannies, even though they suspect that their apartment is located in the middle of a battlefield, in the forgotten Austerlitz of the house interiors. Soldiers decipher wallpaper. A remorseless grammar war is waged in defiance of conventions. Poisonous music is played almost non-stop: even ice violas can be heard, although they are strictly banned by humanitarian pacts. A group of saboteurs managed to insert a new protagonist into the enemy's collection of myths: a demon with deer antlers. Some came with the strange suggestion that the soldiers and the general staff should be told who are the enemies and who are the allies, but that innovation did not meet with any major response: some maintained that it was impossible to tell enemies and allies apart, and others said that there was no difference between them, so there was nothing to identify. A platoon of volunteers is carefully examining a thick book page by page, but they will notice too late a postcard from Salzburg placed between pages 346 and 347; written on it is news about the chilly indifference of puddings, which brings to an end, in no unfortunate manner, the attempts to write a report about the birth of a new divinity in parks. The fallen wander feebly in the erebos of closets; when an invasion takes place in the lobbies and on the night beaches, some of them get drawn in and die once more, finding themselves in an even more distant netherworld, where, on endless plains of waving grass, stand white alabaster locomotives. The remorseless hand-to-hand battles are waged in the intoxicating jungle of the closets; no one knows from behind what hanging suit a sharpened blade will spring out. The soldiers who spend months on end there among the coats themselves end up looking more like coats than people, and their thinking is more like the thinking of coats (for instance, they spend hours on end thinking about a city, where there are houses, monuments and streetlights on springs, and through whose streets there walks a solitary pony). It then happens that the owner of the apartment, when his mind is elsewhere, accidentally dons one of the soldiers and goes out into the street with him. The soldier feels affronted by this and wants to shoot, but his soft rifle merely emits softened bullets that roll along the sidewalk and are pecked at by pigeons. It takes the professional eye of a cloakroom attendant to identify the tragic mistake; she immediately realizes what has happened: she has to be constantly on the look-out because they are always bringing her soldiers and other beings to the cloakroom instead of coats; they have been transferred to closets for some reason, either religious or gastronomic (intoxicatingly sweet fruits ripening in the fall on coat lapels), and in time they come to resemble coats; she knows that if she were to relax her vigilance for a second and hang a false coat in her cloakroom, it might start to bring the other coats to life and they would start crawling around the café and even out the door. The cloakroom attendant would then have to chase after them and would not have

42

time to write her essay about gnoseological dunes. (She is actually a woman of wisdom who used to be consulted by the foremost modern philosophers when they were at a loss. She used to tell them: 'Metaphysically speaking the most important thing in a book of philosophy is the font in which it is typeset: the thickness or slenderness of the letters or the shape of their serifs – the claws that letters use to seize the eye – carry the basic message about the cosmos' – and the philosophers would be amazed at the depth and originality of her thinking.) Now the cloakroom attendants have already emigrated to the secret Greenland at the other end of the cloakrooms, where many of the fallen from the war within the houses wander in forts. On this eve of the Great Fish Feast and not far from the places where it will take place, let us honor their memories in the traditional manner."

They all took little wooden caskets out of their bags and placed them on the desk in front of them. Then they removed the lids. There was a rustling sound and weasels stuck their heads out of the caskets, rested their forelegs on the front side of the caskets and started to hiss. The listeners stood to attention; so did I. Although there was little light in the lecture room, the people standing alongside me soon noticed that I had no animal hissing in front of me. A scandalized whispering spread around the room and soon the entire auditorium was staring at me. I put my bag on the desk and started nervously to pretend I was looking for a casket with its weasel, but then I thought I had better run for the door and I dashed out of the room. I ran down a long dark corridor; at the end of it I looked back and saw the door of the lecture room open slightly and a confusion of weasels tumbled out of it and set off after me. I ran through the darkness and could hear behind me the pattering of many little feet on the stone floor. That's great, I thought to myself, for five years I walked these corridors and some of my erstwhile fellow students teach here during the day, yet here am I being chased along the corridors at night by some animals. On the staircase I managed to increase my lead and I rushed out of the building. But while I was still running through the colonnade the weasels all leaned against the door until it opened and they were tearing after me again. I ran down Kaprova Street. In front of the lit window of the bookshop on the corner of Žatecká Street the weasels outflanked me and formed a complete circle around me. They didn't attack me but whenever I tried to break through the encirclement, one of them would give me a painful bite in the leg.

In a while two other weasels came running from the Arts Faculty. They could not run so fast as they were attached to some harness or other and dragging a small sleigh behind them. On the sleigh stood a television set to which a video camera was attached. The screen bore the grinning face of the man who had been giving the lecture in the dark lecture room. When the sleigh stopped he said in mocking tones: "There is an old proverb that says: 'You won't fry a weasel in a flying cathedral' – if you had only given some thought to the meaning of those words you needn't have ended up in this shameful situation – a situation, which maybe one day will be the subject of a monumental sculptural group depicting you, the weasels and the sleigh with the television, and will be placed at the top of a cliff overlooking the ocean: the television screen which will have a 400-inch diagonal and will shine at night like a lighthouse to distant ships, whose crews largely consist already of sea monsters, because it is increasingly difficult to find seamen – they can't get used to the principle extensively proclaimed nowadays that ships should basically not seek the sea but should take it with them. One seaman told me confidentially just recently: 'I appreciate that it's essential for us to shift our gardens, gazebos and tangled shrubberies about with us, but bringing our own sea along with us? It would be like wanting to

44

breakfast on the monadology at six in the morning, when a quiet scraping can be heard through the wall, as women's hard wing-cases rub against each other in the elevator.' "

At that moment I heard the sound of panting behind me. I turned and saw two more weasels running from the Old Town Square. They also were harnessed to a sleigh on which a television set and video camera bounced up and down. They ran up to us and stopped so suddenly that the sleigh continued on its way and thumped into them from behind, thrusting the weasels muzzle first into the snow. Another face frowned from their screen. It was the face of the man who had preached in the underground temple. The two television screens faced each other and the light from them spilled onto the soiled snow. The priest rounded on the lecturer: "What can you possibly mean by this, my dear friend? Everyone is preparing for tomorrow's festival. They are all run off their feet while you are here amusing yourself! The machines once more have visions, the monks have got hold of some aspic in which there are no butterflies, tortoises are running around the carpets with blasphemous inscriptions set in diamond letters in their shells, no one has thawed the angel of the night, and here you are chatting about seamen and sea monsters! I expect you have forgotten the time when you yourself were still a sea monster and were rifling the kiosks on the coast at night at the head of a gang of the drowned."

But the historian was not going to be intimidated. "I'm gratified that you've remembered me," he said caustically. "I think it's probably the first time since I saved your life, when you were depressed and wanted to eat the plants growing out of forgotten piano keyboards."

"What nonsense are you spouting?!" the priest roared. "The keyboards were long since frozen into the ice and music had been taken over by the night and light, flying drapery."

45

Reproaches and oaths started to come from the television sets. At the same time the weasels harnessed to the sleighs bared their teeth and hissed at each other. They approached each other threateningly, dragging the televisions behind them. Suddenly they pounced and sunk their teeth into each other, at which moment the television sets tumbled over into the snow. The other weasels could not bear to look on idly and divided into two camps, one siding with the priest's animals, the other with the historian's. Eventually a confused tangle of little furry bodies was turning over and over in the snow, biting and mewling. When I saw that no one was taking any notice of me I walked away down Žatecká Street.

# Chapter 7
# The Festival

The following night I walked around the Old Town, hoping I would come upon the festival, about which the historian and the priest had quarreled on the television screens. I walked down Paris Avenue to the Old Town Square. There were no lamps alight and the windows of all the houses were dark. I walked across the square. In the silence all that could be heard was the crunch of the snow beneath my shoes. As I came nearer to the Týn School, I caught sight of something huge and transparent slowly emerging in front of me from Celetná Street with a rattling sound. I jumped aside and hid myself in the impenetrable darkness of the colonnade. When the sliding thing moved forward a bit more I could see it was one of the big glass sculptural groups that had shone in the underground temple. The statue depicted the hero embracing a young girl by a slender pillar, to which was attached a turtle from whose shell there grew long spines, on the points of which was impaled the body of a man in a magnificent robe; there a crown set with gemstones that had rolled from his forehead and lay on the ground by the impassive snout of the turtle. The statue stood on an enormous sleigh; fluorescent fish, disturbed by the jolts, swam back and forth in confusion between the glass figures. Soon there appeared a group of people who were pushing the sleigh: they all wore black masks with pointed, unusually elongated, upturned edges that stuck out either side and ended in silver prongs. The mummers had a red cord with tassels on each end wound several times round their waist and tied in a knot in front; thrust into each of the cords was a crossbow and a heavy hammer. Another statue appeared immediately after the first. It depicted a man kneeling on one knee and gazing intently inside an enormous shining crystal. A third statue recorded a dramatic moment in a duel: one of the duelers had fallen on the ground and let go of his sword, the other's arm was raised to strike the final blow, but was prevented from doing so by a curious dog-headed angel swooping down headlong from above and in mid-flight sinking its teeth in the dueler's wrist. As the sleigh turned into the square the angel's glass foot struck the building on the corner and cracked; a trickle of water started to run from the crack and quickly froze into an icicle. Each of the thirteen statues-cum-aquaria arrived on the square in succession and the mummers arranged them in a circle on the snow between the Týn Church and the Town Hall. The luminous creatures swimming inside the statues shed a pale, restless light on the snow; the glow from the fish also flickered on the façades of the houses. The dark tower of the Town Hall rose above the circle of glass statues that radiated a ghostly glow.

The group of mummers started to perform a silent mystery play about the suffering, death and resurrection of some cruel, young god. I didn't fully grasp the meaning of the actors' exalted gestures, but it seemed to me that the play was about journeying through the jungle, wandering through bustling ports and lethargic palace courtyards in the blistering noonday sun, and despair in gardens at evening. At the moment when, on the hot marble of the quayside, where the chains of the galleys softly jingled, the pieces of the body torn by the tiger came together again and the confused soul, represented by a woman in a fox skin, returned from the underworld, the mummers all broke into a loud cheer and fell upon the statues, which they started to smash to pieces with hammers. Water squirted out in powerful jets and shards of glass fell onto the snow along with fish and sea creatures. Filled with terror they flapped here and there in the snow trying to escape. But the masked figures now pulled out their crossbows and fired at the floundering bodies with metal harpoons attached to strong, fine ropes. The air was filled with the merry shouting of the hunters, the rattle of the ropes flying in an arc, and the slapping sound of the fishes' bodies. A horrified tuna fish flopped up onto the monument to Jan Hus and hid among the stone figures, but even there it could not evade the sharp point of a harpoon. Near me some kind of mottled fish forced itself into a drainpipe and its fins could be heard rattling inside. Some of the creatures tried to save themselves by burrowing into the snow: the trembling tail fins of fish, writhing octopus tentacles and undulating wings of flying fish protruded from the snow like bizarre plants. Here and there the snow glowed mysteriously: it was where fluorescent fish had managed to bury themselves in the snow with their fins. The festival participants shot at the glowing patches in the snow; after the shot the light went out and dark blood started to ooze up to the surface from below. An octopus was creeping over the façade of the Kinsky Palace, gripping onto protruding Rococo ornaments with its tentacles. It was already on the roof and climbing into a dormer window when a harpoon passed through its body; the creature rolled down the steep roof and fell into the square. For a long time, snow went on spilling onto it from the roof. Some of the fish did manage to escape, however. I caught sight of a big shark disappearing into Železná Street; it moved through the snow by alternately flexing and extending its body like a caterpillar. A little while later the bloody frolic abated. The masked individuals gathered the dead fish into nets and set off with them in the direction of Kaprova Street.

The square was once more deserted and silent. I stepped out of the colonnade and walked alone through the blood-soaked snow. I noticed that not far from me the snow was moving: a huge ray fish was wandering in confusion about the empty square, moving by undulating its flat body and stirring up the snow in the process.

I followed in the path of the festival's participants. The bloody stains on the snow showed me the way. I caught up with the fisher people on Marian Square. They had already removed their masks and were unwinding the red cords. There was no longer any trace of their former glee. They stood calmly and in an orderly fashion in a long crooked line, holding nets of dead fish in their hands. I couldn't see what they were actually waiting for, but I joined the end of the line nevertheless. It turned out that we were waiting in line for a ski tow. There were dozens of pairs of skis leaning against the wall of the Clementinum; everyone in the line received a pair; when they had attached the skis, they caught hold of a T-bar coming down the narrow Seminary Lane, then leaned against the bar. I also attached my skis when my turn arrived and leaned against the bar; the rope drew tight and jolted; the skis started to move in the grooves already worn into the snow.

At the end of the short and winding Seminary Lane, the tow turned through the side gate into the Clementinum. I slowly glided through two courtyards (the ski tracks ran so close to the statue of the student defending Prague against the Swedes that its stone plinth grazed the side of my ski). I passed through the open gate into Crusaders' Square, where I was dazzled by the headlights of a late cab and heard the squeal of brakes. Then the T-bar drew me beneath the vaulting of the bridge tower onto Charles Bridge. I slowly moved along the line of snow-covered statues in the straight groove worn by those who preceded me. On the side of Petřín Hill snow shone through the dark trees. Silence reigned. Only when I passed the quickly erected, light-weight poles of the ski-tow structure did I hear a click above my head and the almost inaudible squeak of the swaying empty T-bars that emerged out of the darkness and returned in the opposite direction. The ski tow pulled me along Bridge Street and through the deserted Malá Strana Square where dark cars were parked. I ascended Neruda Street past the closed palace gateways and then the ski tow turned into a passageway and I quietly slid through a labyrinth of narrow backyards, past trash cans and piles of plywood boxes. The T-bar dragged me up cold, dankly-reeking staircases of houses, lit by solitary light bulbs. I passed through dim hallways into a lobby. I shouted out when a figure suddenly appeared in front of me, but it was only my reflection in a big mirror above the shoe rack. I moved through the corners of bedrooms where people lay asleep. A man and a young woman were making love on a wide white bed; the girl heard the clatter and turned her head toward me, silently staring me in the eyes until I disappeared behind the closet. I was traveling through the interspace between the apartments whose existence is denied. I discovered that the apartments are mutually linked by secret trails and passes that run behind the furniture – an entire labyrinth of roads, tunnels and trade routes winding through the depths of the house, through the space that we have proved unable to subdue and annex to our world; so we have preferred to deny its existence. We will pay dearly for our stupid arrogance vis-à-vis those silent spaces one day when shining animals will drive us from our homes and we will be forced to wander these dark trails. I discovered that apartments are much bigger than we imagine, that the dwelling areas and known spaces constitute only a small part, that the totality of the apartment includes dank stone halls whose walls are covered in dreary frescoes, paradise gardens overgrown with luxuriant vegetation, and atria, in whose midst the cold water of fountains gushes high into the air. The secret spaces are linked with the living areas of the apartment by camouflaged passages in nooks and crannies and behind wardrobes, but usually we never set foot in them in our lives – and yet we sense that the decisions whereby our lives are transformed and renewed ripen in the breath that wafts from these places whose existence we deny.

I emerged from the labyrinth of apartments and passageways via an open gateway at the bottom end of Pohořelec Square. I once more caught sight of the festival participants. They had already unfastened their skis and were standing around in clusters holding steaming paper cups in their hands. The ski-tow cable ran into the door of a chapel standing at the top end of the square. Alongside the chapel the white canvas walls of a large tent billowed in the wind. The T-bar pulled me into the chapel through its open doors. The chapel was dark inside and was more reminiscent of a freight car than a sacred building; in the gloom at the end of the building an altar came into view. In front of it the ski-tow winch rotated with a regular creaking. The altar shone palely; as I came closer I could see it was smothered with fish bodies. There were so many fish that they fell from the sides onto the floor, where some of the bodies would flounder for a moment before stiffening. As I approached the winch I threw aside my T-bar and skied out of the tent.

Someone immediately tapped me on the back. I turned round and saw in front of me a bearded man in a long gray coat. I recognized him as one of the two men who had carried my table companion from the Malá Strana Café on a stretcher into the marble streetcar. He must be one of the stewards, because pinned to his sleeve was an arm-band with a grinning piranha fish painted on it.

"How come you arrived without a fish?" he asked gloomily. Why are they always wanting me to carry some animal with me? "I'm afraid a dog jumped on me in the front hall, tore the fish out of my hands and ran off with it," I said.

"You'll have to come with me for a moment," the man said in icy tones. He gripped me firmly under the armpit and dragged me through the huddles of people toward the white tent. I slid awkwardly up the slope alongside him on my slippery skis.

A lamp shone in the middle of the tent and projected the profiles of two figures onto the front canvas wall of the tent. One of them was seated calmly at a desk and writing something, the other, who had a prominently pointed chin, stood in front of the desk, bowing, wriggling and nodding. Their conversation could be heard through the thin canvas. The wriggling and bowing figure groaned: "Please forgive me, Eminence. My behavior was terrible, irresponsible, unforgivable. I answered you back and impertinently asserted that I had saved your life. Of course I know everything I have to thank you for: when I first made your acquaintance I was a mere sea creature and knew nothing about life on dry land. I thought more with my branchia than my head and associated with the drowned and similar riffraff and was not a jot better than any of them. Where would I be now but for you, who pulled me out of the moral mire and extricated me from the seaweed . . ."

"All right, all right, we'll talk about it later," the seated shadow replied, sullenly cutting him short. The sinister steward continued to grip me firmly with one hand while unbuttoning the canvas entrance vent (the buttons were sewn round with the white cotton twine, like the buttons used on duvet or pillow cases) and dragging me into the tent. I could now see that the figure wriggling in front of the desk was the nocturnal lecturer from the Arts Faculty and the seated figure was the man who had preached in the underground temple about the return of the monsters and had berated the lecturer from the television screen shining in the snow in the darkness of Kaprova Street.

"What's the problem?" the seated man asked wearily, when he caught sight of us in the tent entrance. "Someone using banned verbal tenses again? Give me a break, you know they're planning to authorize all the other tenses soon, or at least the white monster tense and the jungle tense. The ban was utterly nonsensical anyway. It's been obvious to everyone for a long time now that all verbal endings are totally harmless and have nothing to do with the evil music that destroys shiny machines."

It looked as if my companion was suddenly too shy to tell why he'd brought me. "He . . . he didn't have a fish," he finally blurted out quietly with downcast eyes. Then he blushed.

The historian staggered and had to prop himself up with the desk. I expect he recognized me because he whispered disconsolately to himself, "No weasel, no fish, nothing. Nothing at all." His whisper turned into quiet sobbing. The features of the sea creature he once was seemed to return to his pain-distorted face: his eyes bulged and the eyelids stiffened. His mouth became round and I soon had the impression that a big fish was gazing at me.

The accusation seemed to have little effect on the seated priest, however. He simply put down his pen and stared at me in silence with an expression of evil amusement. I started to regret not having left the book in the purple binding standing on the shelf in the antiquarian bookshop. The steward became more and more embarrassed, trembling and staring at the toes of his boots. I felt his grip slacken; I tore myself away and skied out of the tent, slaloming between the groups of fishers. Soon I was at the top of Úvoz Street and zoomed down it, bent double. In order to confuse the pursuers I turned off into the darkness of the Strahov Gardens and descended the snowy slope. I stopped among the trees and looked upward, but there was no movement anywhere and no sound broke the silence.

# Chapter 8
## The Bistro at Pohořelec

Can there really exist a world in such close proximity to our own, one that seethes with such strange life, one that was possibly here before our own city and yet we know absolutely nothing about it? The more I pondered on it, the more I was inclined to think that it was indeed quite possible, that it corresponded to our lifestyle, to the way we lived in circumscribed spaces that we are afraid to leave. We are troubled by the dark music heard from over the border, which undermines our order. We fear what looms in the twilit corners; we don't know whether they are broken or disintegrating shapes of our world, or the embryos of a new fauna, which will one day transform the city into its hunting ground – the vanguard of an army of monsters slowly lurking its way through our apartments. That is why we prefer not to see shapes that came into existence on the other side and we don't hear sounds emitted at night beyond the walls. We truly acknowledge only what has taken root in our world, what is connected with the other things and events of those few games we repeat monotonously, and we speak of their internal relationships as if they were the cause, the reason, the meaning. These games that form the tissue of our world are no less strange or horrifying than the nocturnal revelries of the glass statues. And if someone looks from the other side, such as through the gaps between the books in our bookshelf, they must experience the same feelings of unsettling amazement at the fascinating and oppressive rituality, which I experienced when I watched the fish pageant from the colonnade. "What fantastic monsters!" they whisper as they watch us with dread and gloomy admiration.

And yet the world we have confined ourselves in is so narrow. Even inside the space we regard as our property there are places that lie beyond our power, lairs inhabited by creatures whose home is over the border. We are familiar with the strange queasiness we feel when we encounter the reverse side of things and their inner cavities, which refuse to take part in our game: when we shove aside a cabinet during spring-cleaning and suddenly find ourselves looking at the ironically impassive face of its reverse side, which stares into dark chambers that are mirrored on its surface, when we unscrew the back of the television set and run our fingers over the tangle of wires, when we crawl under the bed for a pencil that rolled away and we suddenly find ourselves in a mysterious cavern, whose walls are covered in magical, trembling wisps of dust, a cavern in which something evil is slowly maturing until one quiet afternoon it will emerge into the light. All that exists for us is what forms part of the games we play: it is not surprising that we know nothing about the world that lies beyond the territory of these games; we probably wouldn't notice it even it held its celebrations right in the middle of our daily bustle.

I recalled how the researcher at the library had told me that we cannot see what lives outside the borders, because the beings from over there draw sustenance from another source of meaning and therefore elude our gaze. But I increasingly came to believe that that invisibility was rather the result of how effectively we had managed to repress our gaze and the meager range we had permitted it. The severity with which we rein in our eyes tends to prove that we are aware that our vision dimly understands the monsters of the fringes and we are afraid of their meeting with familiar monsters and starting a conversation with them, or even recalling old friendships and a forgotten common tongue.

The following morning I set off for Pohořelec, to see what remained after the nighttime events, but I came across nothing to suggest that just a few hours ago a chapel, a tent, and a ski tow had stood here. I discovered nothing that was not firmly fixed in the harmonious daylight world. At this early hour of the day the little square was almost deserted; the tourists that would soon flood into it were still at breakfast at the hotels in the city below. The sharp icy wind of elevated spaces blew here and cars stood abandoned in frozen snowdrifts, their roofs covered in hard snow. The bistro with the large window was already open; I suddenly felt like a hot coffee and went inside.

I found myself in a long, narrow room. The front area was bathed in the soft light from the window facing the snow-covered square. At the back, above the bar, pictures of sandy beaches and dewy glasses shone in the gloom. Opposite each other at a small table sat two old ladies who clearly lived locally and came here to have their morning coffee. I sat down in my favorite seat in cafés and bistros: by a window offering chilly vistas and at a small table where the empty chair opposite stares at me like a quiet and understanding animal.

I looked out of the window at the square. Suddenly, from above me there came a pleasant male voice asking me what I would like to order: the waiter had arrived at my table so quietly that I had not even heard his footsteps. I turned my head and looked up into the inclined face of the waiter, who was standing close to my chair. I saw that it was the man who had served mass in the underground temple, who had berated the historian from the mobile television set and before whom I had been taken by the steward for not having a fish. So my escape through the park on skis had been pointless: my pursuer was able to wait for me in the comfort of the bistro and sip sweet, colored liqueurs. I had not managed to elude him after all. The waiter-priest did not pounce on me, however. He did not alter his polite expression but continued to bend over me in an obliging manner. Somewhat perplexed I ordered a coffee and the waiter went over to the bar.

My coffee was brought by a frail lady in a dark dress. When she placed the small nickel-silver tray with the cup of coffee on the table, her arms in their long sleeves reminded me of animals that had cautiously crept out of their lair into the daylight and are ready to run straight back inside in a flash at the first sound of any suspicious rustle. I couldn't help asking her: "Does your waiter have a liking for nighttime festivities?"

The coffee cup that she was still holding on its tray quietly rattled. "He's my husband," she said uneasily. She glanced towards the bar, and when she saw that the waiter had disappeared through the kitchen door, she said in a voice that betrayed a kind of long maturing distress: "Please tell me where you met my husband at night." I asked her to sit in the empty chair at my table and told her the story of the Petřín temple, the television sets in Kaprova Street and the fish festival. She turned her face to the window and looked out at the white square, where two beige-colored poodles were chasing each other.

"I don't know what to do," she said eventually. "My husband is a citizen of some strange city. He has never told me, even though we have lived together for twenty-six years. He has never admitted it even at our most intimate moments, and I have never asked him about it. But I am always finding traces of that other city in corners of the apartment and in the depths of the furniture: little statues of gods with grim expressions on their faces, little gadgets in the shape of birds and tortoises that buzz from time to time and little red bulbs set into their eyes flash on and off, books printed in a strange alphabet with illustrations that shine in rainbow colors and depict temples in the jungle and tigers. When my husband goes out for an evening I know he's going to some sinister ceremony. I don't know anything about his city. Is it a labyrinth of dens lined with gold, an endless palace spreading through hidden places between apartments, a circle of yurts growing up at night on a plain, or a collective hallucination? I don't even know if my husband is a king in his city or a servant. But I think he must occupy some important office, because sometimes I have found newspapers from the other city with his photo in them. I have never been in the other city, although I sense it is nearby, within reach, beyond the walls. Sometimes I hear its voices in the quiet of the night, the distant hum of its boulevards, the chiming of bells, promenade concerts. I think that somewhere beyond the walls in unacknowledged parts of the house there is some hidden sea. I can sometimes hear the sound of ships' sirens and surf breaking against a rock."

I slowly drank my coffee and listened to her sad tale. The first groups of tourists were starting to appear on the snowy sidewalk, and several diplomatic cars crossed the square, heading for the Foreign Ministry. "I have longed all my life for a real home. Meanwhile I live in the anteroom of an incomprehensible temple, whose stench penetrates the cracks in the furniture and pervades every object. There are moments when I shrink from touching even the most ordinary thing. I have the feeling that someone has only lent it to us for a while and that I use it for an entirely different purpose than what was intended for it. I hoped, particularly after the birth of our daughter, that my husband would forget the other city, that in time his life would be integrated into the life of the family, that his role in the family would cease to be for him a role he plays in order to return to his home beyond the walls . . . And then I realized that for my husband the other city had a force of attraction that was far stronger than family bonds. In the end I reconciled myself to solitude and comforted myself with the thought that I had a daughter, who fortunately had nothing in common with the other city. I know her entire life and I don't think it has any hidden corners. She is a well-behaved girl and is studying Czech and physical education at the pedagogical faculty, and she helps me here when she has a spare moment . . . But just recently I've been becoming increasingly anxious. I have a feeling that an odd conspiracy is being hatched between my husband and our daughter. They are almost always together these days and saying things to each other. I once caught my daughter looking at a book with a strange alphabet. Maybe she had just found it somewhere and opened it by chance. Surely someone who was born in our world and lived here twenty years can't suddenly simply cross the border and become an inhabitant of another space. But even so I lay awake for nights on end worrying . . ."

The kitchen door opened and the waiter appeared in the doorway. He was carrying a tray on which there were two plates with sweet omelettes decorated with whipped cream. He headed straight for the old ladies, but I had the feeling that for a split second he glanced toward my table as he stood in the doorway. His wife immediately fell silent and stood up, turning her attention to a jolly and noisy group of customers, who had just entered the room. I sat for a little while longer in the bistro, but she said no more to me and paid me no attention, not even when her husband was in the kitchen. The waiter walked past my table and apologized that it was cold in the bistro because the central heating was incapable of heating the room when it was so frosty outside. He forced some kind of sticky cream puff on me, which he extolled as the specialty of the house. What sort of faces are we going to make at each other the next time we meet at night? Along what paths and by what walls will he pursue me? What punishment will he mete out to me the next time a guard brings me to him?

I waved my check toward the back of the room. At that very moment the bistro door opened and in rushed a tanned girl with black wavy hair, wearing a brightly-colored nylon ski suit. When she caught sight of my hand with the check she called out: "I'll sort out the customer's check, Mom. There's no need for you to come." "That's kind of you, Klára," came the reply from the back. The girl took the check and spent a long time adding up a coffee and a cream roll. She made a mistake and laughed over it. Eventually she did manage to calculate it all and laid the check in front of me on the table. Under the column of figures on the paper was written in a large, somewhat childish hand: "If you want to find out something about the other city, come tonight at 3 A.M. to the bell tower gallery at St Nicholas's Church in Malá Strana. The church will be open." I paid with a straight face and the girl thanked me cheerfully for the tip and rushed off to her parents at the back. I left the bistro and set off down toward the city.

## Chapter 9
## In the Bell Tower

It was not yet three in the morning when I opened the door of St Nicholas's Church. I walked through the dark nave and climbed the spiral staircase to the gallery of the bell tower. There were high snowdrifts by the wall and virgin snow lay on the stone balustrade. The Castle towered above me. The steep roof of St Vitus's Cathedral shone palely and dreamily in the light of the dazzling full moon. The sky was full of bright stars. Far below lay Malá Strana Square; the dirty yellow light of neon lamps spread over its gentle slope. A taxi crossed the square and disappeared into St Thomas Street. Then nothing moved.

A moment later the gate leading to the staircase opened and in the doorway there appeared the girl from the bistro, wearing a bulky down-filled jacket. The jacket was open; under it she wore a black sweater on which a pearl necklace glinted. She leaned on the stone balustrade; the red light of the transmitter on Petřín Hill shone above her dark hair. "Is another festival going to take place down below?" I asked her. The girl gave no reply, it was impossible to gauge any expression on her face, as there were deep shadows beneath the brows and cheekbones.

"You don't believe that Dargoos's holy body was torn to pieces by a tiger," she suddenly declared, breaking the nocturnal silence, her voice harsh and full of disdain. "You don't believe he wandered in fever through desolate parks or engaged in lengthy disputations on the glistening mosaic of the temple floor with cunning priests, who tried to defeat him by using syllogisms, whose main clause consisted of the burrows of underground horses, and also by distracting his attention, when they constantly pointed their fingers at the troops of ten thousand brown mummies in gleaming golden armor, which happened to be passing through the open door of the temple and kicking up the dust of the road. Why are you poking your nose into our affairs? Just remember: whoever crosses the border becomes entangled in the bent wires that stick out of things that you consider broken and which, in fact, have returned to their original form, as it was etched into the surface of a glass star wandering among the constellations. Whoever seeks to penetrate our city will never return. Their faces will disappear into the interwoven network of fissures on old walls. Their gestures will vanish in the movements of bushes swaying in the wind. Don't imagine you can do us any harm by your impudence. But the fact that you have dared to infiltrate the border areas of our city desecrates the memory of those who, five thousand years ago, and with a cold flame in their eyes, knocked over the statue of the winged dog in a forest clearing, and who then, as usual, became winged dogs themselves a bit. What do you want to find here? Even if you succeeded in reaching the fountains in the inner courtyards of the royal palace and heard their murmur, to which our philosophers listen attentively, even if you were to walk through the halls of the palace library and heavy folios opened in front of you with flaming letters on their black pages, you would understand nothing. How stupid and dull you all are in your city: you've forgotten your original tongue and think that what speaks to you quietly in that language is silence. All you see beyond the borders of your space is chaos, deformation and disintegration. You're so diligent and hard-working, you're always building something, but all your feverish searching for a lost beginning and all your buildings are desperate attempts to revive the golden temples and palaces, whose forms are lodged insistently in a dark corner of your memory – and yet you avoid with trepidation and repulsion the only place where you might encounter the living and true legacy of what you seek – the despised fringes. You don't sense that the dread you feel on the periphery of your world is the beginning of the bliss of return, that death in the jungles of the margins is a shining rebirth. Were you to sit in the middle of a junkyard or a waste tip outside your city and meditate on the shapes that are revealed beneath the decaying and rotting masks, you would come much closer to the secret goal of your journey than by remaining in the bewilderingly turning circle of your plans and fulfillments."

I smiled. "Why do you keep on talking about 'you' and 'your city'? I know that you grew up in our world and a year ago you didn't even know another city existed."

The girl came closer and smiled at me. "I promised you you would see something out of the ordinary." She suddenly cuddled up to me from the side. Then winding one arm round my neck and placing the other on my shoulder, she turned me towards the dark shadow beyond the bend in the gallery. She whispered in my ear with a snicker: "It's there at the back in the shadow. You must go just a little bit further." She leaned on me, pushing me toward the dark side of the gallery, still quietly laughing to herself. With her chin resting on my shoulder she said: "You're not scared, are you? After all, you did want to investigate our city. There's no other way. The tour has to start on the tower."

Her jollity really did make me apprehensive about the darkness around the bend in the gallery, and I sensed that something terrifying lurked there. Even so, I broke free of her embrace and pushed her away, heading alone for the border of the dark shadow. After all, she was right: I had set out on an expedition to the other city. I heard quiet laughter behind me. I arrived at the border between the moonlit areas and the impenetrable darkness. Something in the dark rose from the snow and hit me. A cold body with no arms or legs knocked me to the ground. It lay on me, crushing me with its weight. I saw above me the head of a shark with little eyes on either side, and its teeth glinted white. I tried in vain to throw the shark off me. It snapped at my shoulder, but I managed to jerk out of the way, so that it just tore off a piece of the collar. We wrestled silently in the snow. The brilliant moon shone in my eyes. Light went on in a window in the garret of a house below me. I could see an insomniac going to the kitchen and back. I cried out for help, but only the shark and wicked girl could hear me. A moment later the light went out.

The girl tiptoed toward me and leaned over so that her necklace gently touched my forehead. In a quiet, almost soothing voice, she said: "Throughout your life you have looked at the world through cold glass. You used to love the windows of cafés and trains and the glazed terraces of mountain chalets. We know a lot about you. You felt safe behind the glass; why did you leave your shelter and set off on a journey into the jungle? Customers at the Café Slavia are seldom assaulted by sharks. Why did you set out on your own to a strange city where nobody cares about you? Now the shark will bite off your head and roll it around the gallery of the tower and in our schools little children will learn about you in rhymes and counting games."

The door opened and the waiter appeared in the doorway. The girl slowly stood up and stepped to one side, so that he might view the state of the conflict. The waiter smiled and nodded with satisfaction. The girl left me alone and went over to her father, hugging him and kissing him on the cheek. I could see from below the silhouettes of their bodies pressed together beneath the starry sky. I vowed that if by some miracle I manage to get down from the tower I would never again allow the waiter to persuade me to buy one of his cream rolls. He then took his daughter by the hand and they both disappeared in the dark opening of the open door. I remained alone with the shark in the gallery of the tower above the sleeping city.

We continued to fight in the snow for a long time. I did not manage to throw the shark off me, so I tried at least to prevent it from getting me into a position in which it could bite me. But my strength gradually began to ebb. The beast sensed it and it reared for the final blow. At the moment when the shark raised its mighty body and opened wide its maw so that my head would fit inside, I summoned all my remaining strength, leapt up and leaned against it. In its unstable position the shark lost its balance and fell over the balustrade. Its body fell through the darkness and became impaled on the tall metal cross that was held by one of the stone figures on the parapet of St Nicholas's Church. I watched it writhe in its death throes, thereby impaling itself ever more firmly onto the metal of the cross. Soon the movements ceased and the sagging body of the shark hung from the cross like a nocturnal flag. I staggered down the steps to the church, where I collapsed on the cold floor at the foot of a pillar and fell asleep instantly.

# Chapter 10
## Cold Glass

I was woken in the morning by the voices of tourists. I mingled with the visitors and left the church unobtrusively. It was frosty outside and the sky was a clear blue. The sidewalks and the shop fronts still lay in shadow, although the rising sun shone on the tops of the façades and the snow-covered roofs. I walked down to the lower square along the wall of the church and looked upwards: high above the heads of the pedestrians the body of the shark, impaled on the cross, glittered in the rays of the sun. None of the people walking through the square noticed the dead shark. Of course not, we have excised heights from our space just as we have the dark outskirts. What do we know about the mysterious landscapes of façades that sail above our heads like miraculous islands? If a city of gold, with temples and palaces growing on the roofs, who would notice? Maybe a child who has not yet entered the narrow passage of the meaningful, which we stagger along in pursuit of our images, or someone defeated, who has come out of it because his final goal, whose attraction was enhanced by this passage, has collapsed: maybe the person who strolls along without any goal in the glowing new space opened up by the final defeat will suddenly notice that the façades of houses are pages of books on which are written the message of the departed gods that we vainly sought throughout our lives.

I went to the "U hradeb" milk bar for breakfast. I sat on a high stool by the food counter, cutting up a jelly pancake. I couldn't get out of my mind what Klára had told me about windowpanes in the bell tower gallery. I couldn't entirely agree with her. It was a pity that there had been no opportunity up there to talk about it. I noticed how the pancake squirmed beneath the pressure of the knife edge and how the jelly streamed out of the spiral fissures that opened up at each rearing end of the pancake and fell in thick drops onto the plate, and in my head I worked out what I would have replied to the girl in more favorable circumstances – a staircase joke about Malá Strana battles with sea monsters: "I know the fear of encounters that accompanies us throughout our lives. Every genuine encounter destroys our existing world. What comes from the space beyond the frontiers of our world and destroys it we call monstrous: every genuine encounter is an encounter with a monster. But the conjecture that windowpanes constitute walls of a shelter that protects us from the danger of encounters, and from monsters, is maybe only deception. I would have said that, on the contrary, it is the importunate proximity that dominates our daily lives, which prevents encounters and conceals the monstrous that disrupts our world and brings a strange salvation. Proximity space is a stage on which we see only the roles and masks that are part of the play in which we are performing. Cold windowpanes break down proximity space. They rupture the mesh of goals – the spider's web behind which reality has disappeared. It is through glass that we first see for real: dreamily urgent waves of gestures, in which secret rivers of being appear, the fluctuating and fascinating script of the folds of clothing, whose meaning we start to suspect – the fiery glow of colors at the heart of things. We can only start to encounter those things that we have really seen. Those who sit behind cool windows looking out are not seeking sanctuary but demonstrating that they have the courage to encounter. Only behind glass, which strips existence of its false and tiresome roles, is the monstrous shining cosmos revealed to us: a painful dream and our real home." That was another reason why I thought the waiter's daughter was not entirely correct when she contrasted my life behind glass and my entry into the other city. It is precisely when we are looking through glass that we stop dividing reality into center and periphery, and we start to feel a yearning to know the menacing and enticing shapes that loom indistinctly on the border: what appears to be idle gazing behind the glass is actually the beginning of a journey into another world.

A crumpled, abandoned newspaper lay on the shelf beneath the dining counter: I noticed that it was printed in the same script as the book from the antiquarian booksellers in Karlova Street. When I unfolded it I saw on the first page under the banner headline a photograph of my struggle with the shark in the bell-tower gallery. I could not read the article, of course, but I was struck by the quantity of words and sentences set in bold type: it occurred to me that the typographical layout expressed the agitation and outrage of the author. I did not delude myself that the object of the dark hatred that poured over even into the typeface might be the waiter, his daughter, or the shark. The bold characters seemed to be imprinted on the page with a force that was impatient to crush me. I ate the last mouthful of pancake, then folded the newspaper and put it in my pocket. I now had an urge to visit the bistro at Pohořelec. I looked forward to the waiter's reaction when he discovered I was still alive. Maybe Klára would be there too: we could chat about the metaphysics of windowpanes.

I slowly walked up Neruda Street. When the row of houses ended, the snowy gorge of the Strahov Gardens opened up to my left. It glistened in the sunlight as if an extinguished white light had reawakened in the land. The small cottages, whereby the city invaded the world of the gardens on the slope, shone peacefully like the snow's quiet dreams. Above the frontier between the city and the parks – on other occasions agitated and exhaling anxiety – there reigned a quiet truce. Children were sledding down the slope, their distant voices reverberating clearly through the frosty air. The roofs of the monastery church towers glittered in the sun. In the depths below, the thick dark shrubbery intertwined. Snow fell silently from the branches of trees.

Dazzled by the shining snow, I blundered into the darkness of the bistro and sat down by the window. Shapes started to be revealed in the depths of the room. I made out the waiter standing behind the bar with his daughter. The waiter hurried over and asked if I would be wanting coffee like yesterday. He did not appear in the least surprised or taken aback. The coffee was brought to me by Klára, the mistress of the sharks and the tower: she was wearing the same sweater as the previous night but had already removed the pearl necklace. She seemed just as cheerful and carefree as when first I saw her. There was no mention of the nocturnal combat above the city. When the waiter came and steered the conversation round to cream rolls I recalled the resolution I had made on the tower, but I realized that I actually appreciated the tactful way in which they both seemed to avoid speaking to me about the unpleasantnesses of the night before. Maybe this was just a beginning. Maybe they have already prepared further remarkable manhunts. Maybe father and daughter would now be pursuing me every night around tower galleries and snow-covered roofs at the head of a shoal of predatory fish and then serving me breakfast the next morning with obliging smiles. Maybe the newspapers of their city would publish not only articles about us, but also entire serials and comic strips, in which the waiter and Klára would pursue me from one picture to the next. It suddenly struck me as impolite and in bad taste to raise the matter of the nocturnal struggle and I was grateful to them both for their silence. I even allowed myself to be brought another cream roll. Nevertheless I examined minutely, front and back, the check that Klára wrote me. But it contained nothing but figures. "I didn't make a mistake, did I?" she asked, as I gazed at the check. "I'm awful at figures." I told her everything was perfectly all right, took my bill fold from the pocket ripped by the shark's teeth, and paid. The snow continued to glisten outside the window.

# Chapter 11
## The Store in Maisel Street

In the newspaper that had been lying in the milk bar I had noticed some short texts that seemed to be advertisements, judging by the typographical layout. Alongside one of the texts was the photograph of a store window. There was a signboard fixed above the window in large letters of the other city; however, I immediately recognized the dusty stucco angels above the entrance to a house in Maisel Street. There really was a store in the house. It sold shoes and socks – in the daytime at least. I was not particularly surprised to find a photograph of the shoe store in the newspaper of the other city: by now I had some inkling about the lifestyle of our peculiar neighbors, so it seemed perfectly natural to me that just as lectures on daytime and nighttime arts alternated at the Arts Faculty so the shelves of shops should have daytime and nighttime goods, depending on the hour of the day.

That same night I made my way to Maisel Street. In the corner of the store window there cowered a forgotten sock, as the sole remnant of the daytime world. Otherwise the store window was crammed choc-a-bloc with statuettes that all depicted the now familiar scene of the tiger sinking its teeth into the neck of the young man. The statuettes were made of all kinds of materials – porcelain, wood, glass, plush and gingerbread. Some of the wooden statuettes were mounted on wheels and were obviously mobile: the tiger's lower jaw was fastened to the rest of the head with a hinge and probably opened and closed as it moved. I entered by the glazed door. The room's interior was illuminated by the pale light of a round table lamp of opaque glass standing on a counter at which a white-haired old man was snoozing. All around the room shelves stretched from floor to ceiling, covered in heaps of unidentifiable objects. The light of the lamp was so weak that the outlines of the things on the shelves merged into the darkness. I felt as if I were inside a sunken merchant ship. The furthest corners were submerged in impenetrable darkness.

I started to inspect the things on the shelves. There were glasses on which was painted a kitschy portrait of the smiling waiter from the bistro wearing a chain around his neck from which there hung a diamond sea-horse. There were colored postcards on which I could make out an island amidst a dark blue ocean; in the middle of the island the towers of St Vitus's Cathedral rose above the palms against a cloudless clear sky; a white yacht lay at anchor near a sandy beach, where tanned young people held a carefree party beneath striped parasols. It struck me that sounds were coming from the postcard; I pressed my ear to it and could hear distant quiet laughter, music from a gramophone, the chink of glasses and the shrieks of parrots, as well as people's voices drowned by the roar of the surf. There was something that looked like an inflatable rubber animal with no air in it; I found the little mouthpiece and started to blow into it. Various projections slowly started to come to life, filling out and unsteadily extending themselves: it turned out to be an inflatable colored sculptural group. This time it did not depict a man-eating tiger but a group of warriors with double-edged axes in their belts. They were in a forest clearing surrounded by pine trees engaged in pulling down a golden statue of a winged dog from a high stone plinth inscribed with severely angular letters that contrasted with the script of the other city. (The inhabitants of the other city seem to have a marked fondness for statues – even of statues of statues as in this case. If they believe they still live in the favor of the beginning, as Klára explained on the tower, then what they clearly find fascinating about statues is that they disrupt both time in the same way as an existence that – courageously or out of anxiety? – never strays from the source. And yet in both instances it could be just an illusion: in the same way that the sculpture floats through time and its petrified immutability is simply the slow music of weathering, so also the beginning does not remain fixed but is transformed and becomes in a strange way the consequence of its consequences – just as the intention of speech only emerges from the uttered word, which sounds foreign to the speaker and surprisingly like the voice of a demon.) I took the stopper out of the sculptural group; the trees and the figures started to shrivel and cave in; meanwhile the escaping air passed through a mechanism that trumpeted festive tunes, possibly a passage from something like the My Homeland of the other city. I put the deflated sculptural group back on the shelf. A little further on I caught sight of a glass ball that was filled with a clear liquid; inside there stood the statue of a saint holding a cross in his hand: on the cross the impaled body of a shark moved about with its weight. When I shook the ball, it caused snow to fall inside it; the snow was represented by white granules slowly dropping through the liquid to the bottom.

I reached corners that the light of the lamp did not penetrate. Here and there the sound of rattling, clicking, screeching and soft whistling could be heard from the dark shelves; something started to tick regularly and then suddenly fell silent. I thrust my arm into the shelf up to the elbow and let it wander over the things lying there. My fingers crept over minerals with many sharp edges, smooth and heavy metal cones, appliances on which there moved finely knurled cogs, like iron honeycombs and tangles of wires whose rust stuck to my fingers. Then my hand only fumbled with piles of small eight-pointed stars with small round fruits stuck onto their sharp points. After the stars I came upon regular rows of horizontal disks, which languidly yielded to the slightest touch. But when I removed my finger, the disks quickly returned to their original position. When the disks dipped or came up again, a quiet clatter could be heard from around them. The rows of disks stood one above the other, like a model of some strange staircase that collapsed beneath the feet of the person that ascended them: they were possibly a staircase to some secret shrine, whose purpose was to remind the person arriving that the ascent to the deity was simultaneously a constant descent into the abyss. When my fingers climbed these paradoxical steps they were on the edged of a shallow pit, at the bottom of which they touched some kind of thick mesh; was some creature hidden behind it? I suddenly realized that what I was touching was a typewriter. I pressed one of the keys right down and with my other hand I felt how the type bar reared up strenuously and unsteadily like some weird insect, having many nonsensical joints that straightened and then immediately collapsed, before eventually managing to stop for a moment, sticking up in the air and swaying from side to side, after which all the joints gave way and it collapsed once more. When my hand reached the other side of the machine I heard a soft rasping sound. My fingers quickly rushed back and discovered that the type bar had now extended itself quiveringly of its accord, as if some peculiar memory had been awakened in the typewriter and it was trying to accomplish what it had first performed so pathetically.

Behind the typewriter my hand wandered among something that I first took to be dried fruit, but at the last moment I discovered something moving slightly in its midst. One of the supposed pieces of dried fruit actually attached itself to my hand, clinging to it like a child to its mother and not wanting to let go. I flicked it away and several times I caught it and put it back among the rest of the dried fruit, but each time it rushed back and snuggled into my palm. I touched a closed book lying there; the front cover of the leather binding bore an embossed relief depicting a woman in a veil dancing at the foot of some steep mountains, on the side of which a rock city had been carved out. I started to leaf through the book: the pages became harder and heavier all the time. The importunate piece of dried fruit kept on getting in the way of my fingers, when I inadvertently dropped a heavy page on it I heard a short, muffled squeak; I immediately raised the page but the dried fruit had stopped moving. The pages of the book became more and more heavy and stiff until they eventually turned into wooden boards. I realized that they were actually the paddles of a mill wheel; the wheel gave a jerk and slowly started to turn. I thrust my hand into the cold water that flowed down a plastic chute onto the wooden paddles. The bottom of the mill race was covered in fine sand. My fingers came upon a sort of oval shape, covered with coarse bristles and elastic like a peeled hard-boiled egg. I pulled it out of the water; the thing's skin was so taut that it burst open as soon as I pressed it slightly; my fingers slid inside into something sticky that started to trickle out. A moment later I felt an unpleasant slime leaking into my sleeve. I heard a faint rattle; I soon discovered that it was the sound of the dried fruit, lured by the rotten stink of the juice running out of the ruptured thing, which was creeping towards me across the typewriter keyboard. It soon reached me and covered my hand. I shook it off onto the floor; when it recovered from the fall it started to creep into my trouser leg.

I decided to return to where the light was better. I took a tin toy down from one of the shelves: it was a clockwork demon. When I wound it up, it performed something like a Cossack dance along the shelf. In the process it knocked a heavy ink-well onto the floor. The old man behind the counter woke up and shuffled over to me. He picked up a dancing figurine and pressed it into my hands, saying: "This is the spirit that led me out of the labyrinth of fluttering white curtains. Take it if you like it, you don't have any of our money anyway. I know who you are; I was watching television when they showed a live transmission of your duel with the shark – I was rooting for you all the way. I really envy you; it must have been beautiful to fight with a shark above the town at night. Alas, nothing of the kind has happened to me, apart from the time in my youth at the bottom of the sea when I heard the song of the oysters. It is said that people who hear that song of the oysters, never feel like returning to the surface again: they gradually cease speaking, they live alone on the edge of the submarine city in a dreary hotel room, lying entire days and nights in bed, listening to the rattle of submarine streetcars and watching the seaweed waving in the garden outside the window. I did return, however, and over the years the melody of the oysters has matured into a musical composition for fifty-seven pianists playing on one long keyboard stretching through nocturnal villages, shining in the moonlight in deep orchards. Singing with oysters on the seabed was certainly wonderful, but nothing to compare with fighting with a shark at the top of a tower. But do not be angry with Alweyra. Her intentions were good. She wanted to protect the city from aliens; she hasn't yet realized that they are not aliens but simply lost sons returning. If there existed a single being who was alien to the city, the city would come to an end. Do you understand me?"

"I think so. From what I heard on the tower I have come to realize that your city's justification is that it protects and preserves a beginning that has been forgotten elsewhere. (Although I don't know whether this is some ancient legal code, a musical composition that subsequently solidified into words, a vortex of vapor, a crystal, a pure light, a mathematical equation carved in marble in the inner chamber of a pyramid or a dripping patch on the wall comprising the rudiments of all shapes.) To regard someone as an alien would be to deny the relationship of his existence to that beginning, whatever it might be; the beginning would cease to be the beginning if someone eluded its power. Alweyra is the daughter of the waiter in the bistro at Pohořelec? I thought her name was Klára."

"No one is an alien. Everyone is simply returning. Even the oysters are returning, forming long lines from time to time and invading the cities. Shoals of them clatter quietly through our bedrooms. How delighted I am when I hear in the darkness their lovely shuffling! Of course the oysters are not entirely innocent – sometimes the leader of their pack creeps beneath the bedcover and stabs the sleeper in the side with the thorn on the edge of its shell. Then all the other oysters creep up and smother the paralyzed body, sucking it dry, until only skin and bones remain. In spite of that, it is unjust and cruel to eat them alive, particularly when they cry their hearts out in our mouths. Alweyra's father does indeed serve drinks and meals during the day in the long room at the top of the hill on the opposite bank. He is our high priest. I have no idea what they call Alweyra in your city."

"She did not treat me very nicely," I complained. "She lured me to the tower and set a vicious sea creature upon me. The shark intended to bite my head off and did rip off my jacket pocket and a piece of the collar."

"Forgive her, my boy. We are all so fond of her. She is so studious and pious. She spends days studying the complex Tract on the Lights of Night Trains Reflected in Bookcase Windows. She is soon to be ordained as a priestess of Dargoos. The only ancient tradition that generally interests girls of her age is riding the ski lift during the fish festival, but they don't even bother to dress up properly and come bedecked according to the fashions of your city. I'm sorry you feel Alweyra did you wrong. Look, I'll give you something." He reached to the back of the shelves and brought out a little glass phial filled with a dark green liquid. "Here, take it. Drink some when you feel sad. You'll find it will help you."

A well-built man in a fur hat entered the shop, greeted the shopkeeper courteously and started to explain what he was seeking: "I need something that has shiny scales on its surface, at least on Thursdays or Fridays, with little metal prisms rattling inside it, but not too Gothic. It would be fun if it ran on 220 volts or had gills. It doesn't need to sing, and in fact I would sooner it didn't speak at all. That is not to say that it couldn't squawk from time to time, particularly when a green star of monsters is approaching outside the walls."

The shopkeeper nodded knowingly. When the man stopped he thought for a moment and then said: "Wait a moment, I think I might have something for you." He went into the back room and returned holding a box, but in the doorway he stopped and sighed: "Oh, dear, you said 'not too Gothic,' I'm getting very forgetful." He disappeared into the back room again and reappeared with another box, which he handed to the man: "I think you will be happy with this. You must shake it before use. If that makes it give off electric sparks or it starts to squeak, simply put it for a moment under the seat of a night bus whose route takes it through extensive districts of family homes, where, from dark gazebos can be heard fragments of sentences uttered from time to time by damaged automatic preachers once abandoned here: they are excerpts from sermons about decomposed flowers and the Platonic ideal of the railroad embankment overgrown with dusty bushes."

"The railroad embankment . . ." the customer repeated pensively. "It was on a railroad embankment that we first had the idea of building a discounting bank on the borders of hunting grounds glistening with evil. It would incessantly hurl money into the darkness to feed the intricate jungle of nameless, unforgettable and disgusting deeds proliferating in bedrooms at night."

The customer thanked the old man and paid with a roll of bills on which I glimpsed tigers' heads, and left the store. The shopkeeper sat down behind the counter once more and his head started to sink onto his chest. I suddenly realized that it was the first inhabitant of the other city to treat me kindly; perhaps he could help me in my wandering. "Grandpa," I said quickly, in case he fell asleep, "advise me how I could reach the center of your city. It's very important to me. I have heard something about palace courtyards and fountains."

"But what's the point? By searching for the center you move further away from it. The moment you stop looking for it and you forget about it, you'll discover that you never left it."

"But then everyone would be living in the center," I objected. "How can there be so many centers? After all, you agreed that there has to be only one beginning. You also talked about the return of lost sons and about returning oysters – but returning assumes being at a distance from home, which you now deny."

"There aren't multiple centers, just one center and one beginning, but that beginning is entirely in everything that grew out of it. Return is simply a metaphor; in reality, return is always only a recollection of the fact that we are actually at home, that we never left our home. Cosmogony is the inner history of fire; being is a flame that flared up and will be extinguished one day – how do you intend to separate within the flame what is original and what is derived; how do you intend to seek the center of the flame? The flame is nothing but center . . ."

The old man's head once more sank onto his breast and I heard snoring. I didn't wake him, although there were many other things I wanted to ask him. But shortly afterwards the clock on the wall struck: when the point of the big hand reached the highest point of the clock face, a little square window opened above it and an avalanche of little black balls poured out of it and fell with a clatter onto the floor, rolling away into the darkest corners. The shopkeeper twitched and opened his eyes. I immediately took advantage of it and continued with our debate: "All right. I concede that I can find the center only if I stop looking for it. But the only way that could happen is if I consciously tried to forget about the center or if it went out my mind of its own accord. But in the first case my effort not to think about the center would only be another manifestation of searching for the center and therefore it could have no result, and as far as the second possibility is concerned, my feeling is that I couldn't forget the center so easily: all the connections in my life have cracked; it has become a random chaos with broken fragments sticking out everywhere and constantly lacerating my flesh with their sharp edges; every second is a new and unsupported beginning, when an utterly unknown world, for which I'm totally unprepared, hurtles at me from the darkness; I could hardly forget the lost center when all my open wounds cry out for the unity that gushes from the center."

"You're mistaken; that chaos is perfect unity," the old man whispered and narrowed his eyes. "And the thing that arises completely new at every moment simply lays bare the strongest nexus: the nexus of fervor. Are you sure that the edges of broken things really cause you pain? Learn to bathe in the fire of being, it is so easy. There is no reason to go anywhere or seek anything. You don't even have to seek the state of non-seeking, but if you're already seeking it, it doesn't matter. To seek a state in which we no longer seek is a vicious circle that we cannot escape, of course. So what? Why are you always wanting to escape from somewhere, or gain entrance to something? A vicious circle is just as beautiful as all the rest. Why should a straight line be any better than going in a circle? Everything is so beautiful; the things of your city are so intoxicating: the shoes they sell here in the daytime are so poetic with their dark eyelets, so mysterious, like sacred objects of an extinct civilization . . . I'm not even sure why I replace the goods every evening. I expect it's just an old habit and old habits are also beautiful . . ."

"But Klára, I mean Alweyra, scoffed at me on the tower, saying that the inhabitants of my city can never understand the beginning."

"Yes, I know what Alweyra told you. I saw you on television. You suited each other very well – you'd really make a lovely couple. And that shark, wasn't that beautiful? Alweyra has a lot to learn, of course. How could you understand anything at all, how could you utter the simplest sentence if you hadn't perfectly understood the beginning, if you weren't yourself the beginning, the place where constellations are born . . ."

The old man closed his eyes once more and his head dropped. A moment later the slow murmur of his breathing could be heard, mingled with the soft ticking and clicking from the back of the dark shelves.

# Chapter 12
## Flight

I left the store and walked through the night streets. In Široká Street I caught sight of an ocean liner standing in the snow between two rows of dark façades. Its deck was at the level of the fourth floor and light shone from several round portholes in its black-painted hull. I reached the curved side of the ship and touched the cold steel plate with my hand. I could hear voices from above. I stood back and looked up; I saw two figures appear on deck and lean over the railing. The streetlamp lit their faces from below. It was a young man and a girl. I hid beneath the curve of the steel side and listened to their conversation.

The girl said: "This trip has lasted so long, I'm afraid sometimes we'll never reach our destination. Maybe the captain has lost his way. We've found ourselves in the strangest places. I hate those rows of windows; it frightens me when the windows are dark and the reflections of the lanterns creep across their black glass like lights from the lamps of evil water sprites on the surface of nocturnal wells deep in the forest, but it frightens me even more when light comes on in the windows and large unmoving pieces of furniture can be seen in them, as well as walls painted with weird, disturbing patterns – disembodied heads, with mouths that open and close like flapping fish. When will we finally leave this dismal region? It is much more miserable than glacial fields with fantastical ice floes emerging from the gray mist. No one told us anything about these places when we set sail. I'm sure we're lost. Demons have overtaken us on their swift slender craft and lured us off course. I feel that if, by some miracle, we ever reach our destination, those heavy and indifferent pieces of furniture will still be stuck in us and the meandering wallpaper patterns will overgrow our minds and devour all our thoughts, and all our memories. Perhaps we should try to make contact with the natives. Maybe they would explain to us where we are and show us the way . . ."

"Don't worry," the man's voice said reassuringly. "Don't worry, we have an experienced captain. Apparently his family is one of the oldest and is descended from jaguars. He knows how to steer the ship by the constellations and also by the dusty stucco ornaments on the walls of houses. He converses with wise serpents at night. We have old sacral charts and the most hallowed myths have been embedded into the ship's computer programs as shining axioms. All night long figures flash onto the displays whose faint light illuminates frescoes of winged bulls. I recall how I first set eyes on your body as it was embraced by the captain in accordance with the ancient right of *ius primae noctis*."

"I was so glad that you could be there to hold my hand that time."

"Everything will turn out marvelously, you'll see. There is no point asking the natives for directions; it's bound to be a barbaric and uneducated people – how could we give greater credence to their words than to the sentences whose golden letters have gleamed for a thousand years on the pages of our codices that lie on a crystal table within a room, one of whose walls is a splendid cool waterfall? Besides, the seers who prophesy according to the folds in feather bedcovers and those who predict the future according to the murmur of machines in workshops behind walls in suburbs speak of a triumphal arrival, about how we'll soon be walking in light beach clothes beneath palm trees on white boulevards that descend from the Acropolis to the seashore. The governor will receive us and we will drink tea from delicate porcelain cups in a quiet atrium of his palace. Our past fever will be assuaged by cool sundaes in bedewed goblets, on a terrace where the warm wind from the sea will turn the pages of a colored illustrated magazine. The striped parasols are being unfurled and the thin lemon rounds being sliced . . ."

"I'm afraid. I fear that there is no destination, that there are no white boulevards with palm trees, I fear that there is only the night and flurries of snow whirling in the lamplight, only fragments of dark furniture in lighted windows, only grinning masks on the walls with snow in their mouths . . ."

"Come, my darling, it's time to go back to the cabin. I'll prepare you a hot tub. Maybe tomorrow morning we'll catch sight of the shore, white cliffs . . ."

The voices fell silent. I stood a bit longer beneath the curved side of the ship before continuing my walk through the empty streets. I felt sad. I recalled the glass phial that the old shopkeeper gave me and took it out of my pocket. The light of the streetlamp awoke a green sparkle within it. Was it alcohol, a drug, or poison? I drank half the contents in a single swig. The liquid was thick, sticky and over-sweetened.

A moment later I started to feel a strange lightness. My feet rose from the snow, I flapped my arms several times and I was already levitating. I flew through the deserted streets in the frosty night, past the rows of dark windows that had caused the girl on the deck such sadness. I flew higher: over snowy roofs, past chimneys that emitted thin streams of smoke from stoves going out in the darkness of silent rooms. Then I flew lower once more, soaring low above the cars parked at the edge of the sidewalk. From time to time, the toe of my boot would leave a furrow in the snow lying on their roofs. I flew over traffic signals with a monotonously blinking orange light illuminating the snow on the deserted intersections. I sat on the curved top of a streetlamp and rocked back and forth, before once more taking off and slowly flying along the wall of the Clementinum, turning slightly on my axis, past the long row of monstrous faces that topped the pilasters. I flew across the dark river above the foaming weir. As I passed the church of St Nicholas in Malá Strana I flew around the shark's body, frozen stiff. I flapped my arms more briskly and started to rise above the steep rooftops and the narrow dark backyards in the direction of the Castle.

I was tired by now and I sat down on the ridge of the roof of St Vitus's Cathedral for a short rest. On the courtyard below me a circle of lamps attached to the walls of the palace lit up the snow. The lights of the sleeping city twinkled coldly in the distance. After a while I realized that I was not the only person sitting on the roof. A short way away, in the shadow of the tower, there lounged a young man in a tasseled ski cap, smoking a cigarette. In his other hand he held a cage in which there sat a white bird that resembled a parrot apart from its duck bill. I greeted the stranger and asked him politely whether he often sat on the roof of St Vitus's.

He seemed quite pleased to have someone to chat with. "I come here a couple of times a year," he replied. "I'm not particularly fond of the place, though. I do it for Felix's benefit." He stuck his hand through the bars of the cage and stroked the bird's head. "He misses heights, so from time to time I have to take him to a high roof or a tower, otherwise he becomes depressed, stops eating, and, worst of all, he starts losing his memory."

"Why is it important for the bird to have a good memory?" I asked in astonishment.

"For the very good reason that his memory earns me my living. Felix is a ritual reciter bird. I see you're not from our city. All our children know Felix from an early age."

"I must admit that I really have never heard of reciter birds before."

"A reciter bird is an essential part of a major social occasion in our city. In fact the institution of the reciter bird is already mentioned in the second article of our Constitution. A reciter bird knows by heart the national epic *The Broken Spoon* and can recite prescribed passages from it on ceremonial occasions. The epic tells of the founding of our city in the middle of primeval forest and is longer than *The Iliad* and *The Odyssey* combined."

"Couldn't Felix recite something for me?"

"Of course. For instance, he could recite for you the passage dealing with the place where we are right now."

"The roof of St Vitus's Cathedral?"

"Not exactly, but the top of the hill that the cathedral stands on. Felix: 'Toward evening he arrived . . .'" The bird shifted from one foot to another several times, put its head on one side and started to recite in a rasping voice: "The fringes of the empire, untouched by the laws of the center . . ."

The young man leaped up so abruptly that he almost slid down the side of the steep roof, and I had to grab him by the sleeve. "For heaven's sake, what are you spouting?!" he shouted at Felix. "That's not *The Broken Spoon*!" He turned to me and said apologetically: "I've no idea where he learns such things. One day he'll get me into trouble." Then he again spoke to the bird: "All right. Enough goofing: 'Toward evening he arrived . . .'"

This time the bird started to rasp out the proper text, but recited it with such obvious distaste, and when his master was not looking, he made the vilest grimaces:

"Toward evening he arrived at top of the hill to the cavern mouth,
whose gates of gold were locked; the precious metal shone
in the rays of the sun then sinking into the distant dark forest.
It glowed ruddily like the bleeding head of Dargoos,
when the claws of the tiger sank into his cheeks; his holy blood
fell in drops on the white marble in the noontime glow. His noble
companion wrongly tore her hair on the shaded garden terrace,
foolishly, because a mere touch of the tiger's white fangs
will transform the feeble and confused mortal into a radiant
divinity. Mist rose from the deep forests below the cavern, and
here and there above the trees there rose the little circular roof of a
golden temple where pious maidens tantalized the forest god.
Through the valley there wound a cold river, with the island,
on which surly demons had their homes and rode on the backs of
beetles that are larger than human beings and sing vulgar songs . . ."

"That's enough, Felix," the bird keeper interrupted him. "The exegetes consider that that passage contains a description of the Prague basin at the time when the founder of the city, the chief hero of the epic, arrived here. He was a king's son and the seventh incarnation of Dargoos. At the wedding of his twelve sisters to the neighboring king he absent-mindedly broke a spoon and the king took it as an impolite allusion to something that happened to one of his predecessors, who battled an entire day in the burning sun with an evil plant and thus missed the moment when, on the stone wall of his palace, ants arranged themselves into the words of a sentence that spoke about sleeping on a sun-drenched temple corridor and about the monotonous murmur of fountains on broad, empty squares. The king took umbrage and in retaliation started to scoff at the fact that in our hero's homeland the highest religious authorities were green lizards (which was both true and false, but that is neither here nor there). The tipsy hero grabbed a heavy gold goblet, the sides of which bore a relief depicting a battle of galleys on a lake, and smashed the king's head with it. When he asked the oracle how to purge himself of the murder, the priestess told him that he must immediately leave the kingdom and found a city in the depths of a primeval forest, on the spot where he would see a native speaking an alien language and worshiping the statue of a winged dog standing in a clearing. But I can't relate you the whole story."

"Keeping a reciter bird must be a marvelous job," I said. I took pains to flatter the bird keeper so as to elicit from him some information about the other city, after having failed to advance my investigations with the sleeping pantheistic shopkeeper. "You're bound to have a profound attachment to your ancient poetry."

"Not at all. Why? My personal view is that the entire epic is a fairly unsuccessful forgery from the last century."

"So I fail to understand why you chose this particular profession!"

"Quite simply because high fees are paid for bird recitations on ceremonial occasions, nothing else. And ceremonial occasions occur all the time. The people in our city are like children. They're always celebrating something. They're ridiculous with that folklore of theirs. They're constantly bragging that their ceremonies are secret prototypes of the scheme of things in your world and conceal its forgotten meaning. I have my doubts about that. My guess is that the opposite is more likely to be true: that the web of rituals that holds the life of our city together is simply a topsy turvy reflection of historical events that took place in your world. (With our cult of beginning and repetition, we've never managed to produce any history). The dismal dogmas of our mythology are simply fuzzy imitations and counterfeits of your logical laws. Our people maintain they were here thousands of years before you, but their arrogant assertions are based solely on biased and tasteless legends of dubious provenance. Goodness knows what burrows we had to crawl through in order to settle the fringes and cavities of the space that you constructed. We are parasites on your city. Our myths are created out of the detritus of your thinking. Anyway it doesn't matter in the least. But I see Felix has already fallen asleep and I'll have to go. It was a pleasure meeting you. Perhaps we'll meet again some time."

The bird keeper picked up the cage with Felix in it and quickly disappeared into the darkness. I sat for a while longer on the roof of the cathedral, staring at the mournful lights of the lamps in the distance. Then I soared into the air and continued my flight. But the effects of the levitating fluid had diminished and I flew with difficulty, so that it was more a matter of saving myself from falling by waving my arms. I therefore decided to make a landing in the darkened Stag Moat. My feet sunk into untrodden snow and the dark tops of tall trees met over my head. Snowy banks rose steeply and at the very top the walls and roofs of the Castle loomed black against the sky.

# Chapter 13
## Charles Bridge

The following night I was walking along Bridge Street. An elderly man walked wearily ahead of me. I could make out his loose trousers and his bent back in a padded jacket that resembled the garb of road sweepers in our part of the city. He was pushing a two-wheeled hand-cart that was full of various cans and sacks, from which there protruded the wooden handles of some tools or other. When he reached the bridge, he halted in front of the statue of SS Cosmas and Damian and opened an inconspicuous little door hidden in the plinth. It is odd how I had walked across Charles Bridge almost every day of my life but had never noticed a door in the base of the statue. On the other side of the door was a hollowed-out space from which light emerged and was reflected in the snow. Would a hobgoblin emerge, or the head of a dragon? Or would there spew out a red-hot torrent of lava rising from a subterranean lake?

From the illuminated opening there skipped out a little elk, about twenty inches high, with luminous spatulate antlers. It started to leap about gaily in the snow, trying to stick its head into a sack that probably contained fodder. The man in the padded jacket shooed the elk away with a besom broom that he had pulled out of the cart. He proceeded to sweep out carefully the hollow space on the other side of the open door. He strewed hay inside from the sack and took out of the hollow a bowl into which he poured water from a can and placed it back inside the sculptural group. When he had finished, he pushed the cart on to the next statue, depicting St Wenceslas. Here too he opened a little door in the base of the statue, again revealing an illuminated space from which there again leaped out a miniature elk. The man swept out St Wenceslas' interior, strewed hay inside and poured water into the bowl. This was repeated for all the other statues on the bridge. The doors remained open and the elks that sprang forth from them were able to frolic in the snow during the feeding time.

I observed from a distance the feeder's progress from statue to statue. When I reached the statue of St Augustine I stuck my head inside out of curiosity. I could smell the stench of a stable and see that the entire plinth and statue were hollow. The hollow interior matched the external contours of the statue. The stone turned out to be no more than about an inch thick. The interior was lit by a single light bulb hanging at the top in the hollow head of the Bishop of Hippo. The bowl of water stood in a little alcove formed from the interior of the boot trampling on the heretical tomes of Mani and Valentine. The other city seems full of statues, I thought to myself, and its inhabitants cunningly make use of our statues, transforming them into stabling for their domestic animals. Not only have they settled into the nooks and recesses of our space, they also hollow out new spaces within things, in which we have such confidence, and which we assume to be properly solid. I expect the self-confident gestures we use to delimit our space would soon be undermined if we realized that the shapes we touch with such self-assurance are sometimes no more than thin shells enveloping the dark burrows of strange animals. Yet we must reckon with the fact that this thin surface of things will one day wear through and from the holes that appear in it the inquisitive eyes of the lemurs of the interiors will blink at us.

I concluded that the man in the padded jacket was some employee of the municipal authorities of the other city. Apart from feeding the elks he also seemed to have other duties. His hand cart also contained a bag with folded posters and a metal container in which a liquid adhesive splashed around. He stopped between the statue of St Francis Borgia and the statue of St Christopher and pulled out one of the posters, which he started to unfold. The light from the streetlamp fell on his face and I saw with amazement that it was the man who had told me about the secret door in his mistress' apartment and who had been carried off in mid-sentence by the marble streetcar.

I didn't know what to ask him first. "What is inside the green streetcar? Where did they take you? Did they force you to become their servant? Don't worry, I'll help you escape. Tell me what you saw behind the white door!" He gave me an impassive glance and without saying a word continued with what he was doing. He unfolded a poster and pasted it carefully onto the balustrade of the bridge. Then he moved on with the cart to the statue of St Christopher, where he started to tug a reluctant elk out from inside the statue. I stood in confusion alongside the poster that shone white in the light of the streetlamp. The text of the poster was unusually written in our alphabet. It read: "What is hidden behind the mysterious door? When we die will we become white statues on the islands? Felix, the reciter bird, charged with shoplifting in a supermarket. Physicists ask: did the bridge elks emerge in the first seconds after the Big Bang? The maniac who viciously killed the shark on the tower not yet apprehended. Read about these and other interesting stories in the latest issue of *Golden Claw* magazine, a magazine that celebrates its 3500th year of publication, the magazine that our noble patroness covered her face with when frescoes depicting serpents and shining machines started to appear on the white walls of the palace in the silence of the afternoon."

There were stables in each of the statues on the bridge, apart from the statues of SS Barbara, Margaret and Elizabeth, in which there was a bar instead. Four precariously high bar stools stood in the snow in front of the sculpture. Through the opening in the plinth could be seen the upper torso of a white-jacketed barman and behind him rows of bottles neatly arranged on shelves, while colored bar lights shone in the hollow bodies of the statues above. The man who had been kidnapped in the mysterious streetcar left his cart standing a short distance away and sat down on one of the stools. The barman placed in front of him on the stone counter a glass with a dark liquid, from which fluorescent purple vapor rose. I sat down on the adjacent stool and leaned on the bar with one elbow. With my free hand I tugged the kidnapped man by the sleeve. "So what's the story of the door and that streetcar? Tell me everything, I beg you. It's very important for me to know," I exhorted him. The elk keeper simply turned away and gazed in silence at the dark slope of Petřín. The barman, however, leaned out of the statue and said angrily, "You should be ashamed of yourself, talking to an old man like that! For two pins

I'd punch you in the nose. There are limits to rudeness, you must understand. You're in a respectable establishment here, not some undersea grogshop where drunken octopuses screech. I've been working here for years, and I can remember better days when there were really fine bars in these statues – that was before they started expanding operations on the bridge, with this stupid elk breeding – but I've truly never heard such obscenity."

All the elks that had leaped out of the hollows in the statues now bunched together into a herd and ran through the Old Town bridge tower and across Crusaders' Square before disappearing into Karlova Street. I followed them. Their antlers lit up the snow and shone in the glass of the darkened store fronts. When the elks reached the spot by the entrance to the Clementinum, where Karlova Street widens into a small square, they scattered and started chasing each other in the snow. I was standing by The Snake wine restaurant's big window that reaches to the ground; a low snowdrift crept along its bottom edge. The lights were off inside and reflections of the luminous antlers flickered in the dark glass. In the dim light of the streetlamp I could see that a young woman in a light-colored dress was sitting in a seat on the inside of the window gazing thoughtfully at the square. It was Klára/Alweyra.

# Chapter 14
## The Snake Restaurant

I went inside and sat down alongside Alweyra. I no longer cared whether she had some sharp-toothed creature hidden in the darkness. We sat in silence looking at the little elks frisking in the snow. One half of Alweyra's face was dark, the other was lit up by the reflection of the streetlamps outside. "I am also looking through the glass at cold lights," she said with a weary smile. "I have gone too deep into the forest. I was lured by the fire of the beginnings. When my father showed me the way back I thought I was near my forgotten homeland . . ." She fell silent. The elks made long graceful leaps and their antlers drew lines of light in the darkness. A steam sled arrived from Liliová Street with an organ on it played by a woman in an evening gown that glittered in the lamplight. The sled crossed the snow-covered square and disappeared in the dark bend of Seminary Street. "But it is always immoral to return," Alweyra uttered once more in the darkness. "Love of the beginning is a languidly closingly circle, monotonous incest giving rise to disgust. We will lie on cold sheets gazing in fascination at the glowing geometrical figure hovering in the darkness. In the bedrooms lobsters will crawl over our bodies in search of the ice star hidden in the depths of the house. When we return we always encounter monsters in our childhood bedrooms playing slimy Ludo with figures carved from meat. Whatever made me cross the frontier that twinkled in pale indifference on the carpet in the corner of the bedroom? Yes, the city we lived in was not our real home, but as the philosophy machines in the depth of the forest say: 'It's only possible to live with dignity abroad . . . Homeland, the ancestral field, a fiendish paradise . . . The yearning for the beginning and the home is a monster's trap: once we turn back again it is impossible to halt in time. We realize too late that the home we are returning to is not the familiar home but the primeval forest and swamp that were here before the home, and whose breath permeated the house's foundations, took possession of its atmosphere and cunningly penetrated the order of the home. It eludes us because it has robed itself in the accents and melodies of the laws. But the accents and melodies are what actually predominate within the laws. The home was simply a white image in the dream of the primeval forest. They kill the beginning and the spring is always full of poison. There is nowhere to return to. The most suspect joys of the Lotophagi are purer than the Ithaka at the end of the journey . . ."

The sounds of a married couple's tiff could be heard from one of the darkened windows: an angry man's voice and the hysterically screeching voice of a woman. A balcony door opened and a man in pajamas thrust outside a large nickel-silver statue of a general seated with unsheathed sword on a prancing horse. Then a woman in a nightdress appeared on the balcony and pushed it back into the apartment and slammed the door. Alweyra laid her head on my shoulder and whispered: "In the dark Asia of the nooks an emerald serpent bites its own tail. Dargoos is cruel and feeds on time. He sends armies of statues from the glass stars to the nocturnal staircases of houses. Even if we won the grim war with statues it would be a victory full of disgust that will eventually banish us to unreal, glowing roadhouses. Life will gradually be transformed into a vile, unending celebration. I am disgusted by burdensome immortality in huge halls where curtains flap in tall windows and panthers tread lightly across soft, white carpets. The beginning is something more terrifying than chaos. Chaos is always an accessory to order and belongs to our world, whereas the beginning is . . ." She wearily sought the word that eluded her, while outside the window two young sphinxes appeared, tapped on the glass with their little paws and then ran off tittering, ". . . the beginning is the quiet, feebleminded guffaw of a mad god, from which the Word will be articulated . . ."

I put my arm around her and hugged her to me. Her thick, dark hair stroked my face: I remembered wandering through shrubberies of nocturnal gardens in the summer; there had wafted over me the mysterious and sorrowful scent of unknown bodies approaching from the darkness. The elks were resting in the snow. I could think of nothing to comfort Alweyra. I stroked her hair. All that grew out of the emptiness and darkness was the final comfort that emanates from sympathy – groundless and therefore irrefutable – which oddly binds existences, even when only the lukewarm matter of being remains, tumbling from one shape into another in the dream of time. Sympathy gently touches surfaces even when disgust itself loses meaning in the indifferent undulations of the sea of time. We snuggled up together in silence, two bodies with which something reaches out to the darkness and frost, as atrocious as any of the monsters creeping about the plains of the stars.

From Seminary Street there emerged a sled drawn by a team of six clockwork bakelite dogs. A large key protruded from the back of each of the dogs to wind them up. Their legs, whose joints were held together by screws, moved stiffly but rapidly over the snow with a soft clatter. The sled was painted black and the back of it arched upward to form the backrest of a comfortable seat upholstered in red. Seated in it was Alweyra's father. Beneath an unbuttoned beaver skin coat he was wearing his waiter's outfit, but around his neck there hung a gold chain with a diamond sea-horse dangling from it. The clockwork dogs came to a halt in the middle of the little square, possibly because their drive springs had run down. Their leg movements became slower and more jerky until they eventually stopped altogether. The elks surrounded the dogs and nudged them with their muzzles. The dogs fell inertly into the snow. The waiter restlessly scanned the façades of the buildings with his gaze, apparently trying to penetrate the darkness of the darkened rooms beyond the windows. I crept under the table, drawing Alweyra after me. There came a call that betrayed impatience and anxiety: "Alweyra, where are you hiding? Have you forgotten tomorrow's ceremony, when you'll be initiated as a priestess of Dargoos? You were so much looking forward to it, after all! It's time to get ready. People are crowding the steps to congratulate you. The champagne is already bubbling, the balls of caviar are already rolling and the machines for making cloud statues are already being greased . . ." I gripped Alweyra's hand, but she freed herself from me and stood up silently. She walked past the long windows as if in a dream and left the restaurant. Her father immediately leaped up and ran over to embrace her. He led his daughter to the sled and sat her on the seat, nervously covering her with dark, heavy plaids that had been lying alongside it. Finally he wound up each of the dogs one by one, angrily kicking elks out of the way when they got under his feet, and leaped back into the sled. The sled set off once more and disappeared into the darkened mouth of Liliová Street. Shortly afterwards the elk keeper arrived and the elks ran to him. He counted the animals and herded them back toward Charles Bridge.

# Chapter 15
# The Bedsheets

For a long time I went on sitting at the window, gazing at the deserted little square. My eyelids were starting to droop when I was roused from my trance by the roar of an approaching automobile. I opened my eyes and saw a garbage truck approaching from the direction of the Clam-Gallas Palace. It was entirely of glass: through its transparent sides could be seen a heap of sparkling gold jewelry, over which green snakes were slithering. An illuminated domestic standard lamp on a metal leg stuck up out of the jewels and beneath it stood a white-sheeted bed, on which naked lovers embraced. The truck halted in front of the Blue Pike Tavern and the garbage collectors jumped down from the step at the rear and fetched the trash cans standing on the sidewalk. When the tipping mechanism inverted the trash cans into the truck more jewels tipped out of them and more squirming snakes. The jewels spilled all around the bed and the snakes curled around the leg of the standard lamp. When the couple heard the clatter of the gold, they embraced each other even more tightly and quickened their movements. I closed my eyes again and heard the truck depart, then the sound of it trailed away until it was lost behind walls.

I suddenly heard a distant whirr that got gradually louder. Soon a white helicopter appeared above the little square with a roaring tiger painted on its underside. It flew lower and hovered, swaying at head height above the snow. A powerful searchlight came on in one of its windows and a beam of bright light ranged over the façades of the houses, illuminating the interior of the empty tavern, then swooping upward to the attic and traveling down again, entering the darkened bedrooms. I didn't wait for the light to penetrate the restaurant and disappeared into the interior of the building by the back door.

I passed through a maze of dark corridors, gateways, courtyards and stairs. I halted on a glazed verandah whose windows looked down upon a small snow-covered backyard in which there stood a black frame for beating carpets. I could no longer hear the whirr of the helicopter. Silence reigned apart from the dripping of water into a broken basin from a tap at the end of the verandah and the sound of snoring from behind some door or other. I opened the last door in the row, thinking it would lead me out of the verandah, but instead it turned out to be the door into an apartment. In the dark lobby the stench of coats and boots wafted at me. I then walked through a narrow unlit room until I reached the bedroom. In the window could be seen the silent façade of the house on the opposite side of the street. The apartment was cold and empty. There came a rustling sound and I was so startled that I cried out. But it was only a cat creeping out from somewhere; it sidled up to me and scanned me inquisitively with shining eyes. My gaze fell on a made-up bed and I got the urge to take a little nap. I took off my clothes and slipped beneath the heavy, cold comforter in my underwear.

I lay staring at the row of darkened windows of the house opposite. Then I turned over onto my other side, reaching my arm out into the darkness. My fingers found no wall, however. That disquieted me. Had I found myself once again on the edge of some cavern in whose depths someone lay in wait for me? I knelt on the bed and crawled into the darkness on all fours along the wobbling mattress. The bed did not come to an end, but instead broadened out. I stood up and found myself walking across a soft plain that swayed beneath my bare feet. It was covered in crumpled bedsheets, pillows and comforters that were dimly lit by some kind of polar glow, quivering above the white plain. In its light, the folds of the sheets and crumpled comforters had the appearance of recumbent gryphons and sphinxes. I struggled through the comforters as if through snowdrifts; I would get entangled in them and fall onto the plain, which would soften my fall and start swaying beneath me. Here and there would be heard the breathing of sleepers, mumbling from dreams or shrieking from nightmares, and sometimes my foot would touch the body of a sleeper. A gentle wind began to blow and the plain started to undulate as the bedsheets billowed; their murmur merged with the breathing of the sleepers.

The plain of coverlets started to rise and before me there appeared the slopes covered with bedsheets and comforters. Men and women dressed in pajamas, nightdresses and underwear were skiing down the sheets. I arrived at a glazed building with a steep roof that resembled the Crossroads Diner in the Giant Mountains. In front of the cabin, skis had been thrust into the gaps between the mattresses. The skis were decorated with little flowers, stripes and other comforter-cover patterns. I went inside; people in nightclothes were sitting at small tables. I sat down by the window and looked out at the ski-ers on the slope. I could hear the conversation of two ladies in pink nightdresses seated at the next table:

"Won't you go up to the ridge with us tomorrow?"

"I'm scared to. There has been an avalanche warning. I can never forget how my classmate was buried by an avalanche and lay several hours in the dark beneath a comforter before a rescue dog sniffed her out. While she was there she thought up a poem that spoke about gold motorcycles shining in the awoken brain and about how it was necessary for the vanquished always to have compassion on the vic-tor. The words of that poem about sheep stubbornly migrating from somewhere in the maw of long, thick electric cables into the café of the Hotel Evropa, full of guests, who are saddened by the sheep's behavior, became the subject of a large fresco, in front of which, my brother-in-law, returning from a philosophical congress, where his paper had asserted that the main problem of metaphysics was to be solved along the lines of hazelnut muesli, was set upon by female fish vendors, who punched him in the face and shouted at him: 'A well-concealed network of gold-paved freeways is just as noble as the beast that everyone hunts in piano sonatas! Play a new Snow White, for us!' But even after that he was unable to explain what he actually meant by the main problem of metaphysics."

"That's really sad."

I would like to have penetrated deeper into the mysterious space and tried to climb the mattress mountain, but after a while the slope started to be so steep that I had to give up. I climbed back down and was intending to skirt the mountain range, but the soft mountains of comforters at the bottom of dark depressions rose more and more steeply. I caught the sound of a soft whirring and got jumpy. Blinking red lights appeared above the plain and came rapidly closer. It was the helicopter with the picture of the roaring tiger. I started to run but a moment later I became entangled in the bedsheets and fell onto the mattress. The helicopter came to a stop, hovering low above the plain. The sheets, stirred up by the wind caused by the turning rotor blades, started to rise and perform a crazy dance in the air. I was dazzled by the bright light of the searchlight and a harsh voice rang out, distorted by a megaphone: "You are charged with illegally crossing the Frontier, espionage, willful killing of a sacred shark, and uttering banned vowels. Cease all resistance, lie down on the ground and put your hands behind your head!" I broke into a run, making my way past cold geysers of sheets spurting into the air in the dazzling beam of the searchlight that followed me. The machine-gun on board rang out with a delicate sound resembling a carillon. The bullets tore into the pillows and comforters and clouds of feathers rose out of the tears and hovered among the undulating bedsheets. As I ran I learned how to make use of the mattress springs to lengthen my stride, and the more heavily I dropped back onto the plain, the higher and further the mattress projected me until I was eventually soaring above piles of comforters and sleeping bodies in arcs dozens of yards wide. The helicopter circled round me, however, and was now flying at me from in front like some huge, repulsive insect. I fell onto a ruffled pillow and watched the helicopter come closer and dive as the bedsheets rose higher and higher. One of them caught in the rotor blades. The helicopter staggered and fell on its side in the comforters. The rotors continued to turn, ripping the bedsheets, comforters and mattress, and hurling feathers, shreds of cloth and bits of foam rubber into the air. Then came the sound of an explosion that was more like a harmonic chord played by dozens of wind instruments, and the helicopter disappeared in cold, blue flames.

I remained lying where I had fallen and slept for a little while. I was so exhausted from the wild chase that I did not have the strength to return to the mountains in search of a pass to penetrate the depths of another space, so I returned to the dark apartment via the bed plain. I got dressed and was about to leave when I suddenly heard vigorous tapping on the window. Felix the reciter bird was standing on the ledge on the other side of the glass. I was delighted to meet him again and I immediately opened the window, but Felix remained outside. He made a bow and started to recite quickly the poem he had tried to perform for me at our first meeting on the roof of St Vitus's Cathedral. He declaimed the verses with disproportionate pathos, emphasizing the passages that he considered of particular significance by waving his wings and wriggling his entire body, so that I was afraid he might fall off the ledge.

"The fringes of the empire, untouched by the laws of the center,
where the slant-eyed barbarian of the plain
sits silently at an inn table with the customs officer,
a land of exile, where the vanquished enjoys an odd victory
on endless rambles alongside the river,
in the dark back rooms of ice-cream parlors on the square
he touches things lightly in a silent and glistening space without
    goals.
The gleam of the afternoon sun on the cabinet and the indistinct
    voices from the garden
become a splendid new history.

What shines through chinks in the order on the fringes
are the remnants of an older power,
forgotten, yet secretly ruling,
even in the brightly-lit halls of the capital,
heard in the rustle of clothes in the half-open door into the next
    room,
in the murmurs that unite the world of sounds
and alone lend meaning to words,
remnants of the power that uses our plans to organize
the monotonous ballet of the primeval forest,
a power listlessly stretching itself in the thicket of our gestures,
which are less visible to us than the golden halls in the heart of the
    mountains.
The fringes from which is heard the long-drawn-out song of the
    specters
that we heard only in the quiet of the night . . ."

As he said this, Felix flapped his wings so hard that he really did
fall off the ledge. There came an awful squawk from below, but luckily the bird managed to handle his fall. Shortly afterward he flew
back up onto the ledge and continued:

"The fringes from which is heard the long-drawn-out song of the
    specters
that we hear only in the quiet of the night,
when it merges with the roar of water being flushed in the second-
    floor toilet
and with the sound of the train on the distant viaducts of despair
to make the cold, unforgettable music

that gives rise to our exact terms: when the lizards
sail in on their white yachts, they will once more vanish into it.
The places we call the fringes are the secret center
on whose fringes we dwell. Nevertheless, Felix the reciter bird,
who has sat on the shoulders of shiny robots that wandered the
    galleries,
declares that this secret center is itself only the fringes
of a more distant center. The last center gleams in a dream
beyond a thousand frontiers and you'll never reach it,
even if, like me, you traveled through all the cafés, where the waiters
pull the snacks from customers' bags and consume them,
so that customers naturally also start to worry somewhat
about the contents of the sarcophagi that they left in the cloak-
    room,
and indeed, when they ask the attendant for them . . ."

The cat silently leapt up onto the window ledge; Felix squawked once more and flew away. I waited for him to return and tell me something else about the fringes or about what happened with the sarcophagi in the cloakrooms, but he did not reappear. So I left the apartment and descended the dark staircase to the lobby on the first floor of the house. Through the lunette above the street door snow could be seen falling in the light of the streetlamps.

## Chapter 16
## The Ray Fish

In the darkness I felt the cold handle of the street door. It creaked open. Snow flew into the dark passage and flicked across my face. I discovered that I had reached St Anne's Square via the interlinked interiors of the houses. Furious barking alternating with whining could be heard from somewhere. I looked around and saw in front of the portal of the disused monastery a dog with bared teeth harrying the ray fish that I had encountered on the Old Town Square and which had seemingly managed to survive the Fish Festival. On the snow the ray fish was dodging the dog's teeth and defending itself by means of electric shocks. Every time the dog received a shock, it whined and jumped back but immediately pounced on the fish once more. The ray fish was evidently extremely exhausted by now and the electric shocks were growing feebler. The dog's assaults became more and more ferocious, however, and the fish was already bleeding in a number of places where its slender body had been torn by the dog's sharp teeth. The unequal combat was clearly nearing its conclusion. I ran over to the site of the struggle and chased the dog away. The exhausted ray fish lay silently in the snow, bleeding from its wounds while gazing at me with an expression full of gratitude. I stroked its cold body. I had with me a small flat bottle of schnapps and was about to give the ray fish a drink of it when I had a better idea. I took out of my pocket the small phial that still contained the remains of the flying potion. I carefully raised the ray fish and held the phial to the mouth on the underside of its body. "Take a drink," I told it. "It'll do you good." The fish ravenously gulped down the rest of the green liquid.

As the potion started to take effect, the ray fish instinctively knew what to do. It rippled the fringes of its body and took to the air, gliding gracefully around the square at the level of the third floor before landing once more on the snow at my feet. The liquid had obviously given it renewed energy and even its wounds had stopped bleeding. The fish did not fly away, however, but kept returning to me, always landing near my feet and looking at me in a somewhat impatient way. It struck me that it was urging me to do something. I suddenly grasped his meaning. I cautiously climbed onto the creature's flat back and crossed my legs Turkish style. The ray fish delightedly rippled the edges of its body and rose with me into the air.

I was once more sailing through slowly falling snowflakes above the city submerged in darkness. The night was already abating and the first pedestrians from my part of the city were starting to appear on the streets. The ray fish began to climb by means of sweeping curves and soon we were flying into clouds. We emerged above them beneath stars that were already growing pale. The ray fish glided higher and higher while below us the dark sea of clouds unfolded, starting to become clearer in the east. Soon the top of a red sun appeared on the horizon and its rays suddenly lit up the plain of clouds, turning it pink; the black shadows of the folds of the slowly changing waves became pink also. The ray fish flew slowly over the pink sea and I settled myself comfortably on its back, uncorking the schnapps and taking a sip of it. My only regret was that the ray fish had both eyes on the top of its body and could not see the beautiful sunrise above the clouds.

The ray fish slowly started to lose height. It was now flying with me toward the sun, low above the pink surface of the clouds and picking up speed. Ahead of us two pillars of clouds slowly rose above the plain, they both assumed the form of statues of horseback warriors wielding lances. The statues were as tall as a five-story building and were facing us. These were probably the cloud statues of which Alweyra's father had spoken; artists in the other city had apparently mastered some technology allowing them to create statues out of vapor. The two statues slowly changed: the rider on the left turned into a pyramid, with balls fixed to its points – the same solid as on the nine of hearts – the rider on the right remained but his horse's head turned into the head of a beautiful woman gazing in our direction with a dreamy smile. Eventually the two cloud statues stretched upward to form two vertical outstretched arms, each of which held an inverted rabbit's skin in its clenched hand. (What could the unknown sculptor have been trying to say?) The red sun glowed low above the horizon between the two gigantic arms that cast shadows across the entire pink plain. The ray fish was now flying at an incredible speed above the clouds aiming straight between the arms that were coming closer and growing bigger, until we flew through their spectral gateway. I looked back and saw how they gradually collapsed behind us and sank back into the sea of clouds.

The ray fish slowed down and started to descend. The effects of the flying potion were probably wearing off. We plunged once more into the clouds and shortly afterward the roofs of the city appeared, covered in snow. It had stopped snowing and the streets were full of people. As we flew around the gallery of the Malá Strana bridge tower I glimpsed between its columns the grinning face of the waiter, Alweyra's father. The muzzle of a rifle appeared from the shadows. "Watch out!" I shouted, but at that moment a shot rang out. The ray fish staggered and blood spurted from its spine. Malicious laughter came from the tower. The ray fish fell in a steep spiral toward the river. A few yards above Kampa Park I slipped off its back and fell into a pile of snow raked up at the edge of the footpath. The ray fish disappeared beneath the surface of the river, never to reappear again.

I spent the whole day walking aimlessly around the streets. By the afternoon I found myself in a suburb where groups of children were playing in the snow between the long, straight façades of old apartment houses. There was a railroad station nearby from which could be heard the wail of locomotives and the clunk of metal buffers. I found a seat in a tavern, whose windows looked out onto a gray factory wall that extended the entire length of the other side of the street. The Formica tops of the empty tables had a subdued gleam. The only other customers were three pot-bellied drinkers watching an ice-hockey match on a color television screen standing on a shelf on the wall. The barman was sitting with them. He stood up and brought me a beer, then went back and joined the fat men in commenting on the match.

The outlines of the television picture suddenly became sharper and became double. The sound disappeared and from time to time a fuzzy signal from some other station appeared. "It's playing up again! This TV's no damn use, Václav! When are you gonna get it fixed?" one of the customers said morosely to the bartender. The latter retorted: "The repairman was here yesterday. He can't understand what's the matter with it. There must be some powerful transmitter nearby that causes interference." He went over to the television and started to thump it with his fist. After the third blow the ice-hockey stadium disappeared entirely and a clear picture appeared on the screen showing some large interior lit by artificial lighting. I was not even surprised to recognize it as the interior of the underground temple at Petřín. Every single seat in the temple was occupied and in the aisles between two rows of seats television cameras moved up and down on dollies. They were decorated with the same convulsively contorted ornaments as those that crept over the temple walls. In front of the altar stood a glass tank about five feet tall. It was full to the brim with a golden liquid and a step-ladder had been placed at its front edge. At the left of the tank stood the waiter in a magnificent black chasuble with a pink pattern. At the right sat six girls wearing white silk robes embroidered with golden dragons. The last of them was Alweyra.

There came the sound of quiet monotonous music reminiscent of something dripping onto a watery surface. The waiter/high priest donned a ritual cap made of an octopus, which was inverted and probably stiffened inside with wire. Little golden bells had been attached to the tips of the tentacles and their tinkling blended with the soft water music. The portly drinkers burst out laughing and the bar tender slapped his thighs, shouting: "Fantastic. Jeez! Strike me pink!"

The first girl stood up and took off her robe – everyone in the tavern fell silent and started to pay close attention. The naked girl climbed the steps and slipped into the tank. She submerged herself fully and disappeared beneath the surface for about a quarter of a minute. The liquid slowly poured over the side of the vessel: it was apparently honey, dollops of it could be heard plopping onto the floor of the temple. Then the girl surfaced again, blinded by the honey. The waiter gave her his hand and helped her climb out of the tank and descend the steps. She went and stood stiffly at the left of the tank, honey dripping from her caked hair and her entire body. Each of the girls dipped herself in the honey. When Alweyra emerged last from the honey, a close-up of her honey-covered face appeared on the screen. She breathed through her mouth as she had honey up her nose. I had the impression that she was staring at me – but the picture suddenly started to wobble and when it stopped the screen showed an ice rink with hockey players.

"Enough of that," one of the fat men grumbled.

"That was something really stupid again," another of the customers said apropos the broadcast from the underground temple. "Like that time they showed the whale in the lock at Janáček Embankment."

"Sometimes it's quite good," the said bartender in defense of his television. "Such as that slapstick comedy when that loony was fighting on a tower with a shark. That was a real laugh."

I drank another beer and gazed at the ice-hockey match. But the underground temple made no further appearance. I paid and went out into the already darkened street, where snow was starting to fall once more.

# Chapter 17
# The Lock

I set off back in the direction of the city center. I headed down toward
the river past large administrative buildings from the beginning of
the century and alongside railings beyond which snow-covered
parks shone white. A bitter wind was blowing, hurling prickly fine
snow into my face. My eyes were narrowed to slits, through which
the lights of the streetlamps and cars appeared blurred. I walked
along the embankment beneath the bare, black trees. On the other
side of the street was a long row of silent façades with balconies sup-
ported by caryatids. Below me, beneath the iron balustrade, the dark
river flowed, invisible to the eyes of pedestrians hurrying from place
to place, just like the silent life of bodies and like the specters of the
nooks and crannies. I gazed at the dark surface with the swaying
lights. I realized to what extent my vision had changed in recent days.
I laughed: I'm just like the people from the closets and chambers; I
scarcely see anything but the remainder of the world – the fringes

of whose existence no one in my world is even aware, whereas the shapes among which my gaze safely wandered for years are beginning to dissolve in the mist. When will I too turn into a specter?

As I was passing the lock between the embankment and the island I remembered what they had been saying about it in the tavern. I leaned on the cold balustrade and looked downward. Both lock gates were closed and the level of the water between them was the same as the river above the weir. In the shadows a long freight vessel clung to the stone-block wall on the island side of the lock. Its hold contained conical heaps of river sand capped with snow. I could see the dark, empty interior of the raised captain's captain, glazed on all sides. I crossed the bridge to the island and used the metal steps set into the stone wall of the lock to climb down to the deck of the ship.

I mounted some steps into the cabin. Dials blinked and ticked softly on the instrument panel. Through the glazed side of the cabin I could see the wet stones of the wall, as well as the red light above the closed sluice gate that shone onto the snow-covered bushes and the silhouette of the tower by Jirásek Bridge. Suddenly the vessel started to rock. The level of the water in the lock started to fall. I watched as the squared rubble stones were revealed one after another. I shortly realized that the level must have long ago reached the level of the river below the weir. And yet the water went on disappearing somewhere. The gates on either side towered above the surface. They turned out to be standing on stone walls. The vessel quietly descended into an ever-deepening chasm bordered by four walls of basalt blocks. Lights started to glow deep below the surface and gradually rose. Soon some lighted windows emerged, followed by further rows of windows. There were windows in all four walls. Some of them were dark but in most of them there were lights. I could see behind them rooms that scarcely differed from apartments in our own part of the city, except that on the patterned walls of the rooms hung garishly-colored reliefs depicting Dargoos being mauled by the tiger. More and more rooms emerged from the water, rising past the windows of the vessel's cabin and disappearing high above. In one of them a family sat at supper, in another a bald man in a t-shirt was solving a crossword puzzle in the newspaper, in yet another a woman with her hair in a bun was bent over a sewing machine.

After about an hour the vessel came to a halt. I looked upward. I felt as if I was standing in the courtyard of a skyscraper. Above me shone the windows of several dozen floors. The vertical lines converged in a dizzying perspective toward an invisible opening far above, from which tiny flakes of snow fell onto the roof of the cabin. From time to time the light went out in a window somewhere and came on somewhere else. Sometimes one of the windows opened, a dark silhouette appeared in it, and a strident female voice would be heard calling someone. Just above the surface by the side of the vessel I caught sight of the window of an empty and darkened room; a faint light could be seen through the matt pane of glass in a door in the wall opposite the window that led into the adjacent room; the dim light threw the furniture into relief and was reflected in the smooth surfaces of the cupboards and glass. A picture hung on the wall above a heavy leather armchair. In its indistinct blurs I thought I could detect Alweyra's laughing face leaning backward in eddies of streaming hair. I noticed that the window was slightly open and I climbed over from the vessel into the room. I caught the smell of old upholstery and cracked display cases, as well as the sound of scarcely intelligible women's voices coming from the lighted room next door. I tiptoed up to the painting. I had been fooled by the gloom: it was not

Alweyra on the painting; it was not a portrait at all, but an oil painting in a gilt plaster frame (to the bottom of which had been screwed a small oval plate with the number 2092), depicting the modern airy interior of some luxurious villa: through the broad window and the door opening onto the terrace the sea stretched to the sun-drenched horizon. Beyond the terrace, where three wicker chairs were scattered haphazardly about the tiles as if just abandoned by someone, and a tennis racket stood leaning in the corner of a white-painted balustrade, could be seen a rounded bay and a sandy beach where people in swimming costumes lay around languidly in the sun. A hillside rose sleepily from the beach, covered in palm trees and olive groves. Villas swarmed high up the slope, their walls shining white among the foliage. On the wall, perpendicular to the window and the terrace door, hung a dark painting beneath which the lifeless body of a young man in a light-colored suit lay on the floor; leaning over him and mercilessly gnawing his head was a dreadful creature – I was encountering yet again the usual motif of the other city's art, but this time the murderous creature was not a tiger but an ant the size of a grown man. The red blood trickled across the floor and soaked into the tassels of the carpet. In the foreground of the room the anonymous artist had painted a writing desk with several letters scattered on its surface; on the envelope of one of them could be seen a letterhead with the words Société des Bains de Mer. At the edge of the desk a thick book lay open; a ray of light from the adjacent room fell onto this part of the canvas, so I was able to read the text on its pages. It was *The Odyssey* and the line: O moi ego, teon aute broton es gaian ikano – "Alas, what country have I come to now?"; in the margin alongside had been written in tiny letters: "Finally, after many years, the taut string of anguish snapped with a judder, when there unexpectedly appeared in his golden mask, gleaming with venomous reflections of nocturnal lights, He who sings toward morning in the closet. Shapes trembled and burst; what gushed forth upon us came from the lands beyond the furthest frontiers of delight and disgust, from the empty suitcases beneath the bed. Astonishingly it transpired that that infamous lava from the forgotten interiors, slowly rolling over the torn surfaces could have been possibly capable of achieving the unity of the world, of which we had already started to despair in mobile spas, wandering along empty back roads between rows of plum trees. For the first time in our lives it occurred to us that the monsters might be our friends. What did it matter that the cement of that nascent unity would be a stinking slurry? The main thing was that our faces would again be painted on the white pillars standing in the middle of the jungle. Atop them sit green monkeys and from the lake is heard the roar of the jaguar. From today we will approach every shore empty-handed and with a smile that will cause greater offense to the natives than our erstwhile undermining of the laws. It will be fun. Nothing in the world can vanquish our stubborn kindness. The entry *Kindness to monsters*, which will at last mention the quiet tinkle of glasses in display cases in apartments alongside rail tracks, will once more be included in the encyclopedia, alongside a religious picture showing a painfully glittering cathedral of ice. The beasts that wandered in our gestures have been released and now dance every night on the square beneath the bell tower. Nothing can happen to us any more. There is nothing to fear. The gentle touch of a fragrant skin and the brilliant achievement of sharp teeth is part and parcel of that same pageant that spreads from one constellation to another. Let Nausicaa come with her maidens, let a herd of monsters creep up the sand . . ." Here the text ended in a line that ran across the entire page, tearing it at one point. It was probably a vestige of the moment when the person who wrote this strange marginal comment was bitten in the nape of the neck by the giant ant that dragged him away from his desk.

On the picture hanging on the wall above the ant and the young man was a nighttime view of the Main Station in Prague. At the very back, on the last track beneath the hillside, stood a train whose windows were darkened except for one, which emitted a powerful purplish glow. People were coming toward the lighted window across the tangle of rail tracks that reflected the glow from the train and the red and green lights of the signals. They were bearing odd gifts: large stuffed animals and unidentifiable complex machinery. Two railroad workers staggered across the tracks with a large painting depicting the restaurant of the sort of hotel they have in little towns alongside the town hall and the bank; the restaurant, suffused with the dismal light of forenoon, was empty apart from a white-haired gentleman bent over a newspaper, at the very back of one of the booths. On the wall above him hung a smoke-stained painting, which seemed to me to be the same as the one now facing me: the interior of a seaside villa in which a giant ant was killing a young man.

All the time I was examining the painting on the wall and the pictures within it, muffled women's voices and laughter could be heard from beyond the glazed door. I was so absorbed in the paintings that I paid no attention to the sounds coming from the room next door. I suddenly had the impression that someone on the other side of the door had said the name of the street in which I live. I went and stood by the wall next to the door and pressed my ear to the wooden frame. I could hear a woman's voice saying in amusement: "he doesn't even know that the street is part of the long ancient road that runs through cities, forests and plains to the golden palace in the jungle. Most people have forgotten the context of the phases of the path and the direction that gave rise to it and secretly continues to govern it. The path frequently trails away in the landscape and is invisible in the grass. The edges of it merge with the edge of the forest and only very few can distinguish between its moss-covered milestones, which have been worn down by the rain of many centuries, and ordinary stones. Even those who have an inkling of the path's significance start to have their doubts when they have walked for months and years solely through the passages of country taverns with the dank smell of plaster and wobbly tiles, through backyards covered in nettles, along muddy farm tracks and through verandahs with heaps of old junk. They say to themselves, 'these stinking places can hardly be the path to the palace.' When they set out on their journey they had imagined majestic symmetries and vistas between marble columns and now they begin to think they must have lost their way long ago and often give up their search right in front of some moldering door that actually leads to the royal halls."

"Yes," another woman's voice laughed, "the path becomes the right one the very moment when it peters out in the landscape and when we think it no longer leads us onward. At that moment the goal vanishes into thin air. The goal only confuses us on our journey because it is our notion, rooted in the place we started from and constantly drawing us back to it. The only hope we have of reaching the end of the trail is when we forget the goal and the journey, when we enter the space and allow ourselves to be transported by its silent current. The royal palace glitters on the threshold of night between the trunks of the trees when we have long forgotten our dreams about one day setting eyes on it."

"Isn't it funny," a third merry female voice said, "that he doesn't know that the end of the journey governs all its stages? He walks along familiar streets and doesn't know whether he is heading for the golden palace or moving away from it?"

"What's he doing at this moment?" said one of the voices, interrupting the laughter.

"He is in the room next door, looking at the picture." I froze and pressed myself to the wall.

"He's stopped looking at it. He's probably listening at the door now. Do you think he can hear us?"

"Let him listen. He won't understand anything anyway."

"He won't understand. He won't understand," the women's voices chanted gaily. "Just like he didn't understand the message left for him by the Ant-Bitten."

"He's stupid," the voices exulted. "How could he understand the words of the Bitten?"

One of the voices choked as she laughed: "I bet he was spooked by what he saw on the picture. He doesn't suspect that a much bigger insect will live with him for years in his apartment! I think it'll be a big fly."

"A fly! A fly!" the voices called gleefully. Again exultant laughter rang out and the voices started to shout each other down: "It'll live on the books in his bookcases. It'll pull them from the shelves with its proboscis!" "It'll be a faithful companion. When he goes on a trip, it'll follow him down the road. He'll never shoo it away!" "It'll squeeze itself into his compartment on the train!" "When he's visiting a stately home the fly will slide from room to room on the smooth parquet in felt slippers!"

I thrust the door open. The light was on in the room. It was a kitchen with an old dresser painted cream, the surface of which was covered in fine cracks, and a round table covered with a plastic tablecloth. There was nobody in the room. By one wall, on top of an old-fashioned sewing-machine, a record was turning on a gramophone. The record cover, which was propped against the wall, bore a colored photograph of some Alpen hotel. The women's voices were coming from a little speaker that stood alongside the gramophone. They went on yelling something about the fly and laughing, and then the pick-up arm reached the center of the record and stopped. The voices fell silent. I moved the pick-up arm back a few grooves and heard once more ". . . that a much bigger insect will live with him for years in his apartment . . ."

Everything was repeated precisely as before – the same words, the same laughter. I suddenly heard the roar of water and I immediately realized that the level of the water in the lock had started to rise, I dashed back through the kitchen and dark bedroom and leaped onto the parapet of the window, through which water was beginning to pour. At the last moment I caught hold of the disappearing deck and climbed onto the boat. I lay down on a snow-covered pile of sand and gazed upward into a long vertical tunnel through which snow was falling. The laughter of the women from the gramophone fell silent beneath the water, the illuminated windows disappeared beneath the surface and not long afterward the boat was resting once more at the spot where I had first set eyes on it.

# Chapter 18
## The Station

On the Legions Bridge, untrodden, freshly-fallen snow lay twinkling in the light of the streetlamps. I looked around me: the boat with the sand rested calmly in shadow in the lock. I remembered the abandoned train on the picture in the seaside villa and said to myself that I'd try to find it. I set off for the Main Station.

I approached the station from Jerusalem Street. The glazed station concourse shone palely through the dark tree trunks in the snow-covered park. Inside the concourse several people lay sleeping on wooden benches, wrapped up in coats. A cleaning machine with a young man in a light-colored coverall seated on it moved almost silently across the shining floor. I walked through the white-tiled underpass and climbed the stairs to the last platform. Beyond the platform a tangle of tracks shone feebly in the dark yard. Several passengers waiting for the Bratislava express to depart were agitatedly pacing the long platform; the train was already standing on the other side of the platform; the motionless figure of a soldier could be seen through an open window. At a lighted kiosk, whose windows were steamed up from inside, I bought a beer in a paper cup. I leaned my elbow on the counter attached to the side of the kiosk and slowly sipped my beer, while gazing at the web of rails, the lines of which were broken by the black silhouettes of some unfamiliar structures: I couldn't decide whether they were station equipment or some sacred statues from the other city; maybe it was a mixture of the two. I could see on the rearmost tracks motionless passenger and freight trains. Right at the very back, beneath a steep slope overgrown with bushes, stood the train from the painting on the wall of the seaside villa; all its windows were darkened, however. I ducked my head sideways into the narrow window of the kiosk and asked the old woman inside, who was wearing a rabbit-skin vest, if she knew anything about the train on the furthermost track. She started to yell at me to go away, saying she didn't bother to think about such things, that she had enough worries of her own . . . There was a note of anxiety in her voice. I drank the last drop of beer, threw the cup in the trash can and jumped down from the platform onto the tracks. I could hear the agitated voice of the kiosk woman calling to me to come back. I ignored her and blundered my way across the tracks to the dark train in the distance.

The train differed in no way from the other trains. There was nothing to suggest that its dirty windows concealed anything out of the ordinary. I opened the last door of the last car and climbed in up the steps. I walked through the cars past dark empty compartments, with the sound of their windows being gently scraped by branches of bushes growing on the slope. As I was reaching one of

127

the following cars I could see through the glass of the door that its interior consisted of a single room. There were desks in the room at which children were sitting, their backs to me. At the other end of the car a man in a gray jacket sat behind a massive desk rocking on his chair. A young girl stood alongside him. The car obviously served as a classroom. It too was dark inside and the children wrote in their notebooks in luminous ink. I quietly opened the door a fraction. I heard the teacher ask the girl: "Tell me what you know about the origin of case endings."

The pupil started to recite: "Case endings were originally invocations of demons. Each of the modes of human relationship to existence had its own guardian demon. The name of the demon was always invoked after the name of the thing."

"Correct. And now tell us how it came about that invocations of demons turned into case endings."

"Foreign women arrived up the cold staircase with blind jackals . . ."

"Careful. You're mixing it up with the origin of the pluperfect," the teacher interrupted her. "Can't you remember how it was?"

The girl remained silent and nervously shifted from one foot to the other. The teacher turned to the class. "Does anyone else know? How about you?"

He pointed at a boy in the front desk, who stood up and spouted: "When rusty cruisers appeared in the fields of stubble, the names of the demons lost their stress and gradually merged with nouns, and people forgot their original meaning. The connection with the specific type of relationship, which the demon in question had under its control, was transformed into a mere grammatical function."

"Very good. You may sit down. "That's why we say grammar is applied what?" The teacher once more nodded to the girl on the dais.

"Grammar is applied . . . We say that grammar is applied demonology."

"You see, you can if you try. Now tell us what we know about the future development of case endings."

"Case endings will gradually free themselves from their demeaning position and shine once more in their ancient glory. Bit by bit they will separate themselves from the roots of nouns and become what they were at the beginning – the invocation of demons. The roots of nouns will lose their significance and be pronounced more and more quietly, until they eventually become extinct. All that will remain in language are the former endings and people will realize that all the rest is actually superfluous. All that will be heard in the quiet of the halls is the rustling of curtains in the draft and the dreadful names of demons that we now call declension endings."

The girl's voice gradually became more assured, and by the end it seemed to have acquired a sort of maliciously triumphant tone. The teacher listened fascinatedly to the girl. "The rustle of curtains and ancient names . . ." he said with a tremulous voice. "Yes, that will come at the end, but what will come before it? Tell us what will precede it!"

"The monsters' golf course will spread into our bedrooms. A glass pipeline will traverse the maize field and women will run through it in silk underwear at regular intervals. The forests at the dark end of the bedrooms will become impenetrable and white lamps will light up in their depths."

The teacher sat with eyes closed and he clasped the edge of the desk with his outstretched arms. "Yes, yes," he whispered, as if in ecstasy, "at last I'll be able to open my candied encyclopedias and dictionaries and suck all the sweetness from their pages, I will suck and chew them for hours on end in my armchair, dreaming my dreams of switched-on color TV sets slowly flying above an evening meadow on whose screens beautiful animals torment fathers of families. The heavy artillery will return to my apartment at last. Splendid new heresies will be engendered in the wombs of plants and their after-taste will recall bygone nocturnal borsch in glazed diners."

The girl moved closer to the teacher. "Don't fool yourself," she said harshly. "The artillery will never return. They will study in a decaying, incredible Oxford of garbage tips. The candied books will be confiscated and, for the glory of shiny and cruel machines, they will be tossed onto saurians from the reviewing stand (saurians in those days will still parade obediently four abreast, but soon afterward they will conspire with us little girls and declare aloud what has been hushed up for centuries, namely, that dogs have no objective existence)."

"No, that's not possible," the teacher gasped, staring fixedly ahead of him. "That cannot be possible, surely. I spent years trying to transform my typewriter from a gaseous to a liquid state. I purged geometry of polar animals. I introduced cruel polytheism into the city transportation system even though the CEO of the transportation company was initially unsympathetic to the idea and tried to flee me. We chased each other, waving our arms like enormous dragonflies across the surface of lakes from which the song of undines could be softly heard. – Are you trying to say that was all in vain?"

The girl gave an insolent laugh. "Of course it was all in vain, you fool," she said disdainfully. "You purged geometry of polar animals . . . You've forgotten that the first axiom of Euclid states that there will always be one or two penguins in geometrical space? Wasn't it you who tattooed that sentence on my thigh in your automobile of

130

ice? And all the while you were explaining to me that it was that very principle that caused both of Descartes' arms to detach themselves from him and attack him. They set on him like loonies and chased him along the canals and wanted to throw him in the water. In the end he had to flee from them to Queen Christina, but he did not find respite from them even at court, as he admitted in a letter to Arnaud. If, instead of all those nonsensical things you engaged in, you had dimmed your radiance on the chairlift above Špindler's Mill, if you'd seen to it that there were enough functional theological vending machines in the city, if you'd made sure that the barrier behind the glass of your bookshelf was kept lowered . . . As children we also objected to the fact you would visit our homes in the evening and beat our parents with unfritted statues. You turned us against you when we discovered you on the lavatory squeezing oranges onto a pocket calculator. We don't like you and find you ridiculous."

The teacher said nothing but remained sitting at his desk with his head in his hands. There came the sound of children's laughter. The class was mocking its teacher with cruel and hateful laughter, which did not stop, but exploded again and again. I closed the door, returned to the next car, and descended from the train.

I walked along the narrow snow-covered strip between the furthermost track and the overgrown slope. The branches of the bushes chafed my face unpleasantly. Among the bushes on the slope I caught sight of a heavy armored door reminiscent of the entrance to an underground shelter. I strenuously opened the door. Beyond it ran a vaulted passage lined with dirty tiles and lit with light-bulbs that swayed in the draft up under the ceiling. A rusty bicycle was propped up by the wall just inside the door. Down one side of the passage ran some cables and pipes with faucets that had oakum protruding from their joints. On the other wall of the passage pictures had been hung at regular intervals. They were dozens of oil-paintings, all the same size and apparently identical. Each of the paintings depicted the same view of the interior of the seaside villa: it was the same room I had seen on the painting in the apartment below the lock. On these paintings, however, there was no young man, let alone a giant ant. I noticed that a small copper strip had been screwed to the bottom of the frame on all the pictures. On the first painting the strip had a figure one embossed on it and on each of the subsequent pictures the number increased by one. I walked through the gallery of identical paintings in wonderment. But when I then examined the paintings more closely, I discovered details whereby they differed from each other. The folds in the curtains changed and so did the position of people on the beach. Then I noticed that on each picture the second hand of the alarm clock that stood on the desk was a sixtieth of the circle further on than on the previous painting. I realized that the entire gallery was a kind of film which depicted the events in the room at one-second intervals – events that so far consisted solely of the movement of the curtains and the monotonous journey of the second hand around the dial. I went back to the entrance. On the first painting the alarm clock showed precisely twelve o'clock. I mounted the bicycle and started to ride past the paintings.

I rode for almost a mile down the winding passage and all that changed was the shape of the waves and the curtains. Only when I reached the picture with the number 1032 (where the time on the alarm clock was just after 12:15) the head of the ant with its terrible mandibles appeared in the doorway. When the ant saw that there was no one in the room, it scuttled across the room and hid behind the curtains at the side of the window. Pictures 1034 through 1039 showed the individual phases of that move. As I rode past the paintings on the bicycle they really did merge into a sort of movie thriller taking place inside the picture frames. Then for about another half a mile almost nothing happened in the pictures until picture number 1471, where the young man in white clothes entered. In the following pictures he cursorily read his correspondence and then immersed himself in Homer. He underlined the sentence that the exhausted Ulysses says to himself when he is awoken on the shore of the isle of the Phaeacians by the voices of Nausicaa and her companions, and then he started to write his own strange commentary in the margin. The ant crept quietly up behind him and on picture 2054 it sunk its mandibles into the nape of his neck. On the subsequent pictures it dragged him off the chair and hauled him away toward the wall. The picture with the number 2092 was missing: it was the one hanging in the house beneath the lock. The man stopped moving and the ant's mandibles had still not opened, clenched in a spasm of some dark hatred. On picture 2173, a white angel landed on the terrace. He leaped into the room. The ant immediately swooped on him and they fought together furiously on the floor. Meanwhile tanned people continued to bathe carefreely in the waves of the deep blue sea. The ant bit the angel grievously so that golden blood ran from his wounds and glistened in the sunlight. Eventually, however, the angel managed to pin the ant to the floor. He then sat astride it and throttled it until on picture number 2895 its large black feelers stopped twitching. The alarm clock showed 12:40. The angel stood up and started to pull out drawers, feverishly raking through papers. He then removed books from the bookshelves one by one, shaking out the pages, until eventually, from a white booklet whose cover bore the title Hegel et la pensée moderne, séminaire sur Hegel dirigé par Jean Hyppolite au

Collège de France (1967–1968), there fell out onto the floor what he was apparently seeking: oddly enough it was a photograph showing Alweyra and me sitting at the large window of the darkened Snake restaurant. The angel carefully tore the photograph into tiny pieces and then took off from the terrace. He soared above the sea, tossing the fragments of the photograph into the waves and disappearing toward the horizon. By the final painting, which bore the number 3600, the angel had turned into a bright dot above the azure surface of the sea. It was 1 P.M. and on the bay shore the people were exposing their bodies to the sun's burning rays. Beyond that painting the passage ended with a closed door. I leaped down from the bicycle, leaned it against the wall and depressed the door handle.

# Chapter 19
## The Steps

I was standing in a dark room and could once more smell the odor of a strange space, a further chord from the confused and mournful symphony of scents. Through the window I could see the night sky, across which torn clouds scudded restlessly. A clear moon emerged through a gap in them. Its light shone on the wallpaper and glittered on glass in the depths of the room and on the plump leaves of potted plants. Then it went out. I stepped to the window. In the glass a valley swam into view, its relief shattering into countless facets of walls and roofs. I immediately recognized where I was: I must have passed beneath Vinohrady through the winding passage of the gallery and I now found myself in one of the houses standing at the top end of the Nusle Steps and looking through its windows down Nusle Vale. I stood at the window of a strange flat and gazed downward at the dark valley with lamplights glistening in the snow. In the distance the valley sloped up toward Pankrác with its glass hotel tower, whose walls lit up and then went dark again in the changing moonlight.

An adjustable telescope stood on a stand by the window. I placed my eye to the eyepiece and slowly moved the telescope, allowing my gaze to wander over the façades of the houses and along the snow-covered streets. Rows of dark windows appeared in the eyepiece, along with quiet and abandoned trucks, solitary lamps shining in the snow-covered yards of darkened factories, dimly-lit glazed gate-houses, railroad embankments overgrown with impenetrable shrub-bery. Now and then a lighted window would suddenly shine in the eyepiece. I took a look inside an attic bedroom where, beneath the bed, a spring gushed from the floor and ran in a thin stream into the darkness of the recesses; maybe in the other city it joins with other streams bubbling in the darkness and turns into a mighty, slowly rolling river, lined with banks of granite and marble, with stone sphinxes and wide staircases descending below the surface, a river whose murmur we will hear in the quiet of the night beyond the wall. I caught sight of a lobby where mountaineers, ascending some icy peak via a dark and dangerous staircase, were setting up camp beneath a hat stand, on which hung heavy coats. I glimpsed a bedroom with crumpled laundry scattered about armchairs, where some occult celestial pole shone faintly; goodness knows what met-als it agitates and what spikes it attracts to itself in the darkness; an explorer crawled towards it with his last remaining strength across the folds of a carpet that kept curling up, weaving in and out of long white curtains, and clambering over the mountain of crumpled bedding on the unmade bed. I saw a bedroom above the crater of a volcano hidden in the depths of a house; it was irradiated by cool lava shining with a bluish glow that climbed the crevices and slowly flowed from the fissures of the closets, from the gaps between books

136

in the bookcase and the slightly-open drawer of the bedside table alongside a wide bed, on whose dreamily glowing sheets lay two naked girls, enfolding each other in sleep. I saw gamblers at a marble table in an unlit hall of mirrors playing a game with burning cards, whose flames were reflected infinitely in the black darkness of the mirrors, and some sort of somber annunciation, full of venomous effulgences in the window of a dilapidated house above the frozen surface of the Botič river.

I seemed to hear the sound of quiet calling from an open door. I entered the adjacent room: in the front part of the room moonlight lay on a carpet, whose pattern consisted of convoluted arabesques. The rear part of the room, from which came distant anxious cries, was plunged in impenetrable darkness. I stepped right into the room, banging against corners of furniture. I stumbled over a chair and tumbled onto a sprung upholstered couch. The voice fell silent, but a roaring could be heard that became louder and then subsided at regular intervals. Something smooth brushed over my face; I thought it was the touch of some nocturnal insect's wing, but when I reached forward in the darkness I touched some tassels woven into thin cords and hanging from the bottom edge of a cloth lampshade on a tall metal leg. I found the switch cord with a smooth ball at the end and pulled it. An ivory-colored lampshade lit up in the darkness and I saw that the lamp stood on the edge of some sort of cold, forbidding sea and it illuminated the greenish waves that rolled out of the darkness toward my feet. They subsided on the pattern of the carpet and turned to surf that flowed back along the carpet, until it was caught up in a new wave. I could hear the calling once more. In the circle of light from the lamp there appeared a spar with a girl clinging to it; tattered shreds of cloth hung from her body, which was blue with cold. The next wave carried her almost to the white

137

ceiling of the bedroom before depositing her on the carpet in front of me. The girl lay unmoving beneath the lighted lamp. I removed her soaking rags and took her in my arms, placing her beneath the coverlet on the bed right next to the lamp. I pushed the wet hair back from her face: it was the girl I had seen standing on the ship's deck in Široká Street.

I went to the room next-door and lit a gas burner; in the light of it I found a can with a picture of a Chinese dragon and I made her some tea. I came back and sat on the edge of the bed, holding the cup of tea to the girl's lips. When she had drunk it, she looked into my eyes and said in a calm voice: "We were shipwrecked when the ship was sailing through a wild isthmus between bookshelves in some big library. Maybe it struck a reef of petrified books or maybe the sinister, alien programs that had long run rife in the depths of the ship's computers had overrun the navigational plans and cut through the chain of logical implications. It's of little importance now. I was the only one on the ship to be saved . . . I'll never set eyes on my betrothed again. By now he is wandering through cheerless undersea cafés and has only a hazy recollection of the world above the surface, like a strange dream. I realized a long time ago that something evil was being cooked up in the computers, but I was reluctant to talk about it. He had a childlike trust and an unbounded respect for the captain and the crew. I recall his look of reproach when once I couldn't help myself and told him I found the captain disgusting. He wasn't even perturbed when it became obvious to almost all the passengers that at least two of the ship's officers were simply hallucinations and that the passengers' spoilt nighttime dreams were giving birth to some cruel dark Africa ahead of the ship's prow, like a crouching animal ready to pounce on us."

I had the impression that a sea monster was thrusting its horned head out of the sea beyond the bed but it was only an upturned table from the sunken ship bobbing on the crest of a wave. The wave smashed it against an upright piano hidden in the darkness, so that all its strings resounded dully for a long time: a chord from the dark music of madness. "I shall never more feel the touch of his hands," the girl whispered. "I'll only feel the touch of curtains billowing in the draft, or smooth fabric, or the horrible wet leaves of bushes, or the crumbling stucco of walls. Oh God, I'll never get out of this strange, unhappy country. I'll have to live here alone among the motionless figures on the façades and the threatening ornaments on the walls. I will walk along unending walls listening to the sounds of distant trains that are suddenly heard mid-sentence and penetrate the very depths of houses; there is no escaping them . . ."

As if in confirmation of her words there resounded the hoot of a train entering the tunnel – a nocturnal voice of loneliness and despair. I stroked the girl's face. She gripped me by the wrist and drew me to her. With unexpected force she tugged me under the coverlet, pressing her cold body to mine and winding her legs around me. She reached under my shirt with her hands and clenched them firmly at my back. We were lying on our sides and over her shoulder, which had slipped out from under the coverlet, I could see green waves rising in the lamplight, coming closer and then falling away. Now and then drops of spray would fall on the coverlet and our faces. The cold lips rose from the pillow, groped about my face like some sea creature, then enclosed my mouth and clung to it.

I heard footsteps behind me, muffled by the carpet. The girl clung to me even more tightly in apprehension. I tore my mouth away from hers and turned my head. There appeared the outline of a dark figure, approaching hesitantly among the furniture. When the figure entered the circle illuminated by the lamp I could see it was the young man who had stood with the girl on the deck of the ship talking to her about walking on the seashore and bedewed goblets. When the girl recognized him she cried out with joy, but she did not release me immediately, only slowly relaxing her embrace.

"You're still alive! How did you manage to save yourself?" she shouted, while her hand continued to wander to and fro beneath my shirt. "Did you swim to shore on the back of a dolphin? Were you taken aboard by one of the smugglers' boats that wander through the depths of the houses?"

Her friend sat down on the edge of the bed, leaned across me and started to kiss the girl's face, shoulders and breasts. The girl finally withdrew her arm from under my shirt and placed it around her fiancée's neck. I felt awkward and uncomfortable. I turned onto my stomach and tried to crawl beneath their bodies, now enfolding each other. "I wasn't on the ship when it foundered," the man said in his kindly, mellow voice. "When you went to sleep, I went off to the department store to buy you some dates, dried apricots, and cashew nuts." He pulled a cashew nut out of a plastic bag and put it in the girl's mouth. They took no further notice of me. I finally managed to climb out of the bed and crossed the room to the window, in which the moon was shining. Behind me I could still hear their conversation, mixed with the roaring of the waves.

"What will we do?" the girl said. "We'll never reach the island now. We'll never walk along the white promenades or sit on a terrace above the sea . . ."

"It doesn't matter," her friend replied. "It's better this way. We'll imagine it all, and it'll be much more beautiful. Every day we'll dream

140

up excursions, games in gleaming pools, splendid parties with lanterns, flirting with interesting people, dancing at night on the decks of yachts. We're not so dull as to need reality . . ."

The voices in the depths of the room merged with the murmur of the sea. I went out of the apartment into the dark passage. The house door opened directly onto the Nusle Steps. I walked down the snow-covered steps into Nusle Vale. To my left, railroad tracks left the tunnel beneath the hillside and branched out. To my right, shrubs growing on the edge of the snow-covered gardens bent over the wall. My feet cautiously felt for the edge of the steps in the snowdrifts. The moon had disappeared behind the clouds and I was in complete darkness, yet I had the impression of a faint glow growing brighter in the snow. I turned and froze. A figure was descending the steps, slowly, with head bent. From head to foot it emitted a pale greenish glow. It was covered in a snow-white cloak with a wide hood that covered its face. Dark blood was soaking through the white fabric in large patches. I backed toward the garden wall and could feel the bent branches of the shrubs pressing into my back and thrusting into my hair. The glowing figure came closer. When its foot touched the step on which I was standing it stopped and turned its head toward me. It removed the hood and I cried out: I beheld the gaunt face that had gazed on me over recent days from many pictures and statues. I caught sight of the deep neck wound on the neck from which dark blood streamed. "Dargoos," I whispered. We stood face to face gazing silently at each other. Beyond the palely glowing head with its long disheveled hair a night express with lighted windows crossed the viaduct. Blood dripped softly onto the snow. I didn't know how to behave; I'd never met a god before. I almost went up to him and offered my hand. Ought I to ask him to carry the betrothed couple

141

whose ship foundered in the treacherous inner sea to the islands or to help Alweyra in her confusion and distress? Ought I to request him to lead me to his city that constantly eludes me, the city with the squares and palaces? But Dargoos did not look as if he could help anyone. It was not the proud and cruel deity depicted by the statues. His face was that of a fugitive alien, wandering in confusion, like me, through lands of exile. It seemed that his divine existence was enormous unending suffering that could never cease. I felt compassion for him. I'd have loved to do something for him, but I knew there was no way to help him.

Dargoos once more drew the hood across his face and continued his descent. I saw him pass the Excelsior restaurant and turn into the quiet streets between the Nusle Steps and the Botič – an area full of garages with closed shades, blank workshop walls, decaying factories and dusty shrubs alongside the railroad track.

# Chapter 20
# The Jungle

The girl's talk of being shipwrecked among bookshelves recalled what the researcher at the Clementinum had said about the library's dark corners. The next day I went to see him in his office once more and told him all about the other city and my wanderings, requesting him to guide me into the depths of the book depository. He did not like the idea very much; it was obvious that he had long ago lost any desire to visit the precarious periphery of our space and search for the hidden frontiers.

"I think it's time you gave up these expeditions of yours," he told me. "You're already beginning to look like an inhabitant of some phantom city yourself. But if you're determined to reach that other city come what may, then I'd advise you to choose some other route. The path through the library is dangerous. The library is a treacherous place; you'll often find that the spines of books at one end of a bookshelf are lit up by daylight from the window, the din of the street outside can be heard and two librarians have bumped into each other and are chatting about yesterday's television program, while at the other end of the shelf mist is beginning to swirl in the twilight, stinking seaweed hangs from the books and the malevolent snarling of some wild creature rends the air. Even an experienced librarian has been known to over-estimate his knowledge of the library and set off for some under-explored area in search of a book. He is warned by his colleagues not to go there but he just laughs and says he's worked in the library for thirty years and knows every nook and cranny. When he takes no heed of the warnings, the other librarians rush off to find the reader and beg him to cancel his request, bringing him teetering stacks of magnificent books, books with flashing jewels embedded in the binding and pages scented with the rarest perfumes of the Orient, books with three-dimensional illustrations, full of soft velvets and fine sand, books with edible pages tasting of lotus leaves, which the reader may immediately devour after reading, silken books that can be unfolded and used either as a hammock or on windy days as a hovercraft with which to float high above the landscape, books with intoxicatingly erotic stories played out on nocturnal marble terraces beneath cypress trees by the sea: the pages of these books have been soaked in hashish so that after awhile anyone reading the book is gripped by a hallucinatory vision and becomes part of the story, bathing with beautiful girls in the warm nocturnal sea, but the stubborn reader casts not one glance at the books they have brought and insists on his book – a book about car maintenance or making pickles – he wants it because he requested it and believes it to be the duty of the library staff to obtain it for him willy nilly, and to the unfortunate librarian's beautiful daughter whom someone has meanwhile summoned by telephone and who is offering the reader, like Sheherezade, to tell him stories all night long, he merely declares: 'Look here, young lady, there is nothing for us to discuss, I want my book on car maintenance (making pickles)' – and so the librarian embraces his daughter and sets off into the depths of the library, everyone gazing stupefied at his departing figure; at the bend in the corridor he turns and waves before disappearing behind the shelves and no one sets eyes on him again; the reader waits in vain for his book, pangs of conscience start to gnaw at him, every hour he goes to ask whether the librarian has returned with his book and he ends up spending the entire day by the book delivery hatch and by five in the morning is marking time outside the locked doors of the Clementinum intoning dismal dirges. Several librarians disappear in the depths of the library every year and the librarianship schools are unable to turn out enough graduates. Someone has set up a monument to the lost librarians among the bookshelves: it is a bronze statue of a librarian in an overall dying of exhaustion on a pile of books, though even at this moment he retains his sense of duty and his fingers, with their last remaining strength, grip a request form for the book *Überwindung der Metaphysik durch logische Analyse der Sprache*. I don't know how the librarians met their ends, whether they lost their way in the endless passages between bookshelves and died of hunger and thirst or whether they fell prey to wild beasts lurking in the depths of the library. Maybe there are primitive tribes living there who hunt librarians and even eat them: occasionally the distant beat of tom-toms can be heard from the depths of the library and there are some lady librarians who claim to have glimpsed at the end of a passage or in the gap between removed books the painted face of a savage. But it is equally possible that the savages are the wild descendants of the librarians who failed to find their way back out of the library. Are you still determined that I should guide you into the heart of the library?"

"Maybe I'll go wild too and dance among the books to the sound of drums, maybe my face at the end of a passage will scare a lady librarian, but it's too late to turn back now. I must go on. I have got too close to the frontiers of the other city; what wafted from there was enough to undermine the last remnants of the network of customs into whose fabric our entire behavior is woven: without that support, the simplest of actions disintegrate into dozens of separate operations, each of which must be built up separately from the foundations out of nothing and then matched up with the rest; one must consider the thousands of possible relationships that arise thereby, so that lunch in a restaurant or shopping become something akin to the labors of Hercules. I must go on towards the other city; the old order will not bear any more patching; it was always full of holes through which shone the pulsations of primordial currents of some kind. And everything indicates that those currents flow from the other city and my hope is that in its center I will discover the spring that is the source of our order and which alone can renew it. It can't be helped, I must go into the library. I don't know what monsters I shall encounter but I think it will not be any more terrible than life in my own city. And besides, I have prepared myself well for the journey." I opened my rucksack and showed him my stock of food, taking out my torch and brandishing my machete above my head.

The researcher sighed. "All right, if you're incapable of lunching in a restaurant, I will lead you into the library. But I will go with you only as far as the boundary of the danger zone. From there on you must proceed alone. If you don't return, don't expect anyone to come looking for you."

We walked along between endless shelves of books. At first our path took us up straight, well-lit aisles past neatly-arranged volumes but as we penetrated the bowels of the library the books started to disintegrate and torn pages emerged from them. Meanwhile fewer and fewer of the light-bulbs were working so that from time to time we were groping along in darkness. We reached a point where a number of paths crossed. The intersection was lit by a weak bulb; the mouths of the passages which led deeper into the library were dark and gave off the heavy odor of old paper. My guide now halted. "This is where the jungle begins," he said gravely and pointed towards the dark mouths of the aisles between the shelves. "I will leave you here. Good luck, and take care of yourself." He shook me by the hand and left quickly.

I entered one of the narrow aisles. For a while I proceeded in darkness, which was illuminated here and there by the glow of putrefying books. I switched on my torch and let the beam wander over the bookshelves. In the damp air the pages of the books curled, swelled, frayed and turned to pulp, expanding and forcing the bindings outwards, tearing them and squeezing out through the holes. Covers were falling apart and leaves prolapsed from them, lolling out of the books like tired tongues, falling on the ground and mixing with leaves from other books, putrefying and forming a soaring pile of oozing, phosphorescent, malodorous compost, through which I had to force my way waist-deep at times. The wooden shelves on which the books stood cracked and twisted. In the putrefying insides of the books, in dark crannies between the leaves, seeds of plants became fixed and sprouted in the damp darkness, sinking their roots into the paper and thrusting their shoots up to the edge of the book where their agile heads broke their way out, sometimes turning into lianas which hung in elaborate strings around the library and dripped sticky sap, sometimes becoming runners that crept along the shelves, forcing their way into other books, squeezing between the closed pages and fighting their way to the very center to take root there.

On some of the stalks growing from inside the books, heavy, bland-tasting fruit was ripening. What was most nauseating in these stuffy and fetid surroundings was not the realization that a strange accidental calamity was occurring with rampant nature devouring the fruits of the human spirit; what gave rise to increasing anxiety was rather the fact that the dreamlike transformation of books into dangerous and unemotional vegetation laid bare the malignant disease secretly festering in every book and in every sign created by humans. I read somewhere that books treat solely of other books and that signs likewise refer to other signs; that a book has nothing to do with reality, but instead reality itself is a book since it is created by language. What was depressing about that doctrine was that it allowed reality to be hidden by our signs. The realization that wafted from the decaying library was far more somber, however: what I could see here was that books and signs remain rooted in reality and governed by its unknown currents, that our signifying and communicating is embedded in being, which signifies itself, its secret rhythms, and that original signification, that original dull glow of being keeps alive our meanings while at the same time threatening to swallow them again and dissolve them in itself. In the library turned jungle I came to the realization that the letters in those broken books and in a new book on a bookshop counter are simply specks like others with which burgeoning life adorns the surface of existence and with which it merely expresses its monotonous and unintelligible whisper.

In that humid world of collapsing shapes lived various creatures: as I leafed through books I would come across flat mollusks that slid between the pages and that imitated them so well that it was very hard to tell them apart; I usually only discovered the creature when what I thought was a page suddenly curled up at the touch of my fingers and then wriggled off into the darkness: there were times when an apparent book entirely dispersed, being in reality merely a colony of the mollusks stuck together. There seemed to be more and more of the creatures, but in actual fact I was learning to recognize their mimicry which had rendered the creatures invisible to me at first. Their camouflage was often almost perfect, and nature displayed its most brilliant achievement on the bodies of the large newts: the black blemishes on their white skin looked just like letters of the alphabet, so that when a newt was lying on a pile of pages it was invisible. The letters were usually grouped in meaningless combinations, but sometimes by chance there emerged an intelligible word or even part of a sentence laden with some sort of meaning: I read on the skin of newts the words "lascivious," "blenched," "arbitration," and on the tail of one creature I made out the phrase "crystal cursed queen."

This rampant life of the library – the rotting and twisting of shelves, the swelling of books, the aggressive burgeoning of plants, the ripening and rotting of fruit, the pervasion of creatures – meant that the bookcases expanded and became bloated with the constant turmoil; the aisles between them became narrower; I was obliged to squeeze through gulches and cut myself a path through overgrown books with the machete. Sometimes the bookshelves on either side would coalesce, the burgeoning books and the stalks that grew out of them intertwining to form solid bridges that resisted even machete blows; that meant I was forced to crawl through long, narrow tunnels beneath the fused bookshelves: on one occasion in the tunnel the light of the torch fell on the hideous snarling face of a creature as it emerged from the swamp just ahead of me; the beast gave out a piercing shriek and snapped at my face. On another occasion some creature was passing down the tunnel in the same direction as I, and was obviously in a great hurry. I could hear behind me impatient snuffling and grunting and the beast bit me in the heel to hurry me along; finally it started to crawl over me and the weight of it pushed me into the mire, while the animal went on grumbling in annoyance.

The deeper I went into the library the harder it became to distinguish between the leaves of books and the leaves of plants, or tell apart the wood of the bookshelves and the trunks of the trees that grew here out of the fertile book compost. Everything coalesced into a jungle thriving and decaying in the unbearable heat, humidity and stench. I reached the bank of a turbid, slow-flowing river about as wide as the Vltava in Prague. It occurred to me that I could make a raft. I used lianas to lash together a number of fallen tree trunks that were lying in the swamp and found a piece of shelving that could serve as a paddle. I launched the raft onto the river and paddled it into midstream where I allowed myself to be carried along by the sluggish current, shining my torch at each of the banks in turn, but making out in its light only a thicket of shrubs-cum-bookcases arching over the surface of the river and rippling the water with its hanging branches. From time to time there rang out the shriek of a bird or the scream of an animal having its flesh torn by sharp teeth. On either bank rows of tall columns started to emerge from the bush, rising up into pitch black emptiness, and wreathed in creepers that climbed up towards the richly ornamented capitals that held up nothing; there appeared the outer walls of buildings in which the floors had collapsed and an impenetrable thicket held sway. Had the current carried me to some uninhabited, derelict quarter of the other city or was I in the ruined metropolis of a lost empire older still than the city I was seeking? I floated along between the lengthy façades of palaces with bushes thrusting their branches out of the dark holes of their windows. I passed several spacious squares with weeds growing in the crevices between the granite slabs, with massive equestrian monuments eaten away by the roots of climbing plants, and with metal fountains: at first sight I thought that muddy water was cascading in the fountains, but it turned out to be only the thick veils of creepers that grew in the bowls of the fountains and hung out over their sides. Finally the last collapsing wall of all sank into the bushes, the torch lit up several more solitary columns and the uninterrupted thicket lined the banks once again.

I heard a distant roar that grew steadily louder. The current quickened; I realized that I was being drawn towards a mighty waterfall hidden in the darkness. With every ounce of strength I paddled with the broken bookshelf to get the raft to the bank. The roar of falling water became a menacing bellow. The current kept pulling the raft into midstream. At the very last moment I managed to catch hold of an aerial root that jutted out over the surface of the water and scramble along it to the bank. The raft with all my belongings was carried off by the river, leaving me without even a torch. I stood defenseless in total darkness deep in the jungle.

I groped my way blindly down the steep overgrown bank, struggling through bushes in the deafening din of the water as it tumbled alongside me into the depths. When I finally reached the bottom and felt beneath my feet the narrow band of sand that divided the river from the jungle undergrowth I was overcome by such tiredness that I lay down on the damp river bank. The invisible waterfall thundered above me. A moment later I fell asleep.

When I awoke and opened my eyes I cried out in amazement. The jungle on the opposite bank was engulfed in fire. Dazzling flames flared up and illuminated with red light the roaring wall of falling water, taller than a ten-story building, phantom nocturnal organ-pipes. I stood for a long time on the bank staring at the crimson falling waters.

# Chapter 21
## The Temple in the Rock

I continued my journey along the narrow strip of sand. To my left the reflections of the fire shone red on the dark surface of the river, on my right the heavily-scented jungle rubbed against me. Suddenly a rock face loomed up out of the jungle. It was bathed in the ruddy glow of the flames from the opposite bank so that I could see that Dargoos's features had been carved out of the rock in gigantic proportions: they looked exactly as I had seen them on the Nusle Steps – drawn and emaciated with mad eyes. The stone sculpture had been scored through by the water running down the rocks, and the hollows of the mouth and the eyes were overgrown with moss. Just above the sandy bank a crack opened in the rock; running up to it were dilapidated steps with a twisted handrail of metal posts. I climbed the steps and entered the rock.

I found myself in a spacious cave with burning faggots on the walls that illuminated faded frescos depicting battles between some kind of metallic creatures in a nocturnal park behind whose dark trees shone the lights of streetcars. The roof of the cave disappeared in the darkness. In a niche stood an altar made out of a narrow tin locker like the ones used in factory changing-rooms. Inside the locker some sort of sacred objects hung on coat-hangers. In front of the locker-altar a gaunt old man in a primitive garment sewn together roughly out of the pages of books sat crossed-legged muttering some sort of prayer or incantation. Not wanting to disturb his religious observance I waited in embarrassment for him to finish his discourse with the deities. When the old man had finished muttering he turned to me a furrowed, ascetic face: "Have you come for a magic amulet or do you need your fortune told?"

I explained to him that I was coming from a city that lay on the other side of the jungle and that I had got lost. "I visited your city once as a young man," said the guardian of the temple. "That was a long time ago. But what possessed you to undertake such a dangerous journey? You do not look like the sort who make their way into the heart of the jungle in search of the pearls that grow between the pages of books or to hunt the rare shaggy crocodiles whose skins are worth their weight in gold – they all dream of finding fairy-tale treasure in the jungle and end up going out of their minds when the wild forest angels start tailing them and reciting obscene dream epics non-stop, or they are overcome by the burgeoning vegetation; the books they lie down on start to grow into their bodies, the bindings fuse with their skin and the wind riffles the pages that bristle all over their bodies."

I felt I could trust the hermit so I told him the story of the mysterious book found on the shelf of the antiquarian bookseller's and the quest for the other city. He listened to me attentively: when I had finished he beckoned to me to come closer and nodded for me to

153

stoop towards him. Placing his bony hand on my shoulder he drew me closer still. He whispered in my ear: "Your journey was a waste of time, you placed yourself at risk for nothing. I will tell you something . . . But not here, we'll go outside."

I detected disquiet in his whispering. Whose ears did he fear in a cave in the middle of the jungle? Did he think that the deity could hear him by the tin altar or had listening devices been installed in the rocky wall? He took me by the hand and led me out of the cave. We sat down on the sandy shore and leaned our backs against the rock-face. Before us a red strip of fire glowed on the opposite bank reflected in the dark surface of the river.

"You want to discover the city that borders on your city. You want to worm your way right into the very heart of it. You believe it is also the hidden center of your own city and hence an understanding of the laws of the other city could mean renewing the order which you consider ruined . . . What you are seeking you can never find."

The guardian of the temple now spoke more loudly and his voice was calmer than inside the cave. "So I am going in the wrong direction?" I asked. "It's so hard to tell in this jungle. I feel so terribly tired."

"No, the jungle is indeed on the territory of the city that you seek. If you were to continue along the path you would eventually see above the treetops the golden tips of the tower of the royal palace. But the other city also has its periphery, where it passes over to another space. Perhaps you will reach the palace on the main square and maybe you will walk along its passages. Maybe you will reach the royal library and hold in your hands the Book of Laws. But it will not help you. You will find no beginning there: the laws have been copied from the neighbors, who themselves copied them from their neighbors . . . Quiet, didn't you hear a bubbling in the reeds?" All of a sudden there returned to his voice the same anxiety I had observed earlier in the temple.

"It was just some fish or other. I think I've come across that doctrine somewhere else before. I once heard a poem whose author maintains that the secret center that we seek is in reality the edge of another center, which is itself an edge; the final center is supposedly so remote that we have no hope of ever reaching it."

"Whoever told you such things?" the hermit asked in astonishment.

"A reciter bird called Felix lectured me about it one freezing night while falling off the window ledge."

"Oh, Felix. Felix is an old chatter-box. No, what your reciter bird was talking about was in fact another doctrine entirely. It is not at all a question of the center being remote and mediated in too complicated a fashion, nor of the original law being irreparably distorted by countless translations of translations like a game of Chinese whispers, nor yet of the god's face being hidden behind thousands of masks. The curious secret is that there exists no final center, that no face is hidden behind the masks, there is no original word in the game of whispers, no original of the translations. All there is is a constantly turning string of transformations, giving rise to further transformations. There is no city of autochthons. There is an endless chain of cities, a circle without beginning or end over which there breaks unrelentingly a shifting wave of laws. There is the city-jungle and the city where people live in the pillars of tall viaducts that crisscross each other in countless overpasses and underpasses, the city of sounds and nothing else, the city in the swamp, the city of smooth white balls rolling on concrete, the city comprising apartments spread across several continents, the city where sculptures fall endlessly from dark clouds and smash on the paving stones, the city where the moon's path passes through the insides of apartments. All cities are mutually the center and periphery, beginning and end, capital and colony of each other."

"That's an odd doctrine," I said, "I can't make up my mind whether it is conducive to despair or to a strange happiness."

"Happiness and despair are words that have meaning in a world which has beginning and continuation, center and periphery. If you allow yourself to be carried off by the rolling wave you'll forget what they mean and you'll be unable to say whether everything has entirely lost all meaning or whether everything is full of meaning down to the very last atom. Looming before you will be the Labyrinth of collapsed time; in its passages shining in the darkness in regular rows by the brick walls will be slot machines with electronic games about the pursuit of pursuers and you won't know whether you've gone mad or whether you've understood the mystery of the cosmos that has been eluding you your entire life."

On the opposite bank a tall burning trunk was falling quietly in a strange kind of slow motion, a warm wind blew and blotches of red light danced and trembled on the black surface of the river. The guardian of the temple stared at the dancing lights and said in a weary voice: "Don't go anywhere. Every landscape is a beginning and an end, every city is to the same degree both the phantasmagoria of a mad dream and boring reality. The city where you live is no less a dream and hallucination than the city of marble tigers on the malachite plain, on whose flanks dewdrops shine like gemstones, when the red sun rises above the horizon. Return to your dream, sacrifice to the gods of your dream, use dream machines, rotating and vibrating in a bizarre technological dream, in a narcotic, unbelievable ballet. I too am a priest in Dargoos's sanctuary; were I to live in the land beyond the lofty steel-plate walls where the supreme deity is a geometric figure: a beautiful polygon with many axes of symmetry, I would worship that divinity and carve its form in crystal. Return home . . . Alternatively don't go back, and travel instead from city to city, traversing the entire chain of cities. It will amount to the same thing . . ."

Now I too caught the sound of bubbling in the reeds by the bank. A narrow metal spike rose above the surface, waved and disappeared again. Then a head appeared enclosed in a dark rubber helmet, the face concealed by diving goggles and a double snorkel emerging from the mouth. Out of the water stepped a black-suited figure with an oxygen cylinder on its back and holding a long narrow sword. The glow of the fire glistened on its blade. The contours of a female body showed beneath the clinging rubber suit. The diver took off her goggles, removed the snorkel from her mouth, pulled the helmet off her head and shook out her black hair: once again it was Alweyra, standing here with her face twisted with rage and malice. Behind the dark figure glowed the burning jungle, surrounding the wavy hair with a ruddy halo. She made two rapid steps forward in her rubber flippers and placed her sword on the neck of the temple guardian, pressing his head against the rock face with the sharp point.

"We've caught you at last," she hissed at him. "I've taped your heresy, your vile blaspheming against Dargoos. We've long suspected you of being a supporter of the Thousand-City Sect, but had no proof – you were as wily and slippery as a snake. It was our fault that you spread your poison once more. Our attention waned over the past centuries; we thought your perverted teachings died out a thousand years ago when your evil prophet was impaled on a golden screw ... It was only recently that we came across clues that the trampled snake was raising its head once more. We discovered in backyards remnants of your disgusting orgies, the charred remains of sewing machines smeared with redcurrant jelly ..."

She lowered the sword and snapped a shining handcuff onto the temple guardian's wrist, attaching the other manacle to the iron railing. Then she turned to me: "As for you, you've heard too much to be allowed to return to your city." She raised high the ruddily glowing sword; I raced off, running along the narrow riverbank, and where the rock-face receded I plunged into the jungle, thrusting my way through it in the dark, all the while hearing Alweyra cutting a path by hacking furiously at the branches and creepers with her sword. Then just as I felt her sword point in my back, a stone wall blocked my path. I swerved and crawled through the bushes by the wall. After a few yards my hands felt a little door. Pressing down the rusty catch I ran through it and banged the door behind me at the very moment when the sword's nimble point was lunging at me from the doorway.

I found myself in an illuminated windowless room. On a chair opposite me sat a gray-haired lady in a white nylon overall reading a women's magazine. In front of her on a little table lay neatly rolled lengths of toilet paper. I was in the basement toilets at the Slavia Café. I placed a crown piece on the lady's plate and mounted the staircase.

It was dark outside the large windows; the café was full of people. Above the marble tabletops shone the candelabra reflected deceptively in the mirrors and darkened windowpanes. I rushed towards the exit, but then it struck me as rather silly to be evading Alweyra

158

on this side of the frontier, in a world where she was probably powerless. Besides I was exhausted from my wanderings in the jungle and felt like a drink. I sat down at a small empty table near the piano and ordered a cognac from the waitress. I gazed at the staircase leading up from the toilets, straining my ears to hear the slap of rubber flippers on the stairs. I wondered whether Alweyra would emerge in her black diving suit in the brightly lit café, brandishing her slender sword, whose images would glisten in the cold depths of the mirrors. But no one appeared on the stairs; Alweyra respected the frontier between the two cities. She was well brought up and knew that it was impolite to bring into cafés conflicts that originated deep in the jungle, even if their rooms were only separated from the primeval forest and its beasts by the thinnest of walls, just a little door adjacent to the toilets.

# Chapter 22
## Departure

It wasn't only wandering in the jungle that caused my exhaustion. I was tired out from all those attempts to penetrate the other city, to reach its hidden squares and palaces and the sources of its power. I was weary from living on the border: on the border of a homeland, whose events, in which the sap of meaning has dried up, have gradually been changing into a meaningless ritual, and foreign parts whose order constantly eluded me. I had encountered the words and gestures of the inhabitants of the other city, the screeches of its creatures, and the stiff poses of its statues like a hieroglyphic text, whose shapes from time to time have been penetratingly and almost painfully cut through by the incandescent discharge of unifying meaning, but every time it had been extinguished before I managed to grasp it. I led a strange existence between two empires, in one of which the flame of meaning had gone out, while in the other it could still not be kindled. The testimonies I had heard about the other city tended to be perplexing. What Alweyra, the shopkeeper, the bird minder, Felix and the Guardian of the Temple had said about the other city was completely contradictory – and yet it was obvious that all of those explanations were somehow valid.

I had no wish to go anywhere. I sat at home reading a thick book about logic; the clear morning sunlight, refined with reflections of the snow, lay on its pages. Suddenly my eye encountered a strange hybrid word: the first part consisted of letters in Roman script but attached to it, like a mermaid's tail, was a second part made up of letters from the other city. Had some type remained at the bottom of the type case after the nocturnal activity and got picked up by the daytime typesetter by mistake? Were the alien letters a secret message for spies of the other city from their headquarters deep inside the space beyond the walls? I suspected there was another explanation, however. The book I was reading had its place not far from the center of the bookcase in which I had placed the book from the Karlova Street bookshop. I took out some booklet or other that stood even closer to the book with the purple binding and leafed through it. Just as I feared, I discovered on its pages many more letters from the other city; there were actually entire words and fragments of sentences. I anxiously removed a book standing right alongside the mysterious purple volume. When I opened its pages it was like rolling away a flat stone and gazing at beetles as they swarmed about. The pages were almost entirely covered with the thick black letters from over the border; only here and there were there little islands of Roman script. I felt queasy and I slammed the book shut. I now knew for certain where I stood: the alien script had spread throughout the bookcase like mildew. I pulled out the infectious purple book and dashed about the room with it, seeking a place to hide it. Is it possible to cure a bookcase festering with an unintelligible script?

Then I stopped and laughed at my anxiety as I returned the book to the bookcase. Let the rounded and spiny letters proliferate, let tigers come onto the carpet from the dark nooks, let the waves of the denied sea roll into the very center of the rooms from the depths of the houses. What have I to be scared of anymore? I suddenly realized why the other city had not accepted me, I grasped why neither the helicopter's machine guns hovering over the undulating coverlets, nor the sharks in the snowdrifts nor the point of Alweyra's sword had been the real obstacles. All at once I knew that the other city must open up to whoever really wants to leave; then every path they take will lead them to the shining palaces and gardens. I had not really left yet. To really leave one must leave everything behind and go smiling and empty-handed with no thought of return. Those who depart while counting on returning do not leave home, even if they reach the white cities in the depths of the jungle and repose on the marble of its squares: their journeys remain woven into the tissue of the objectives that create the space of home; the shining borders of foreign parts retreat before them. I have lived my whole life on the periphery and have been more at home in the world of stains and cracks on old walls than in the world of shapes acknowledged as meaningful and alone important. I never understood the purpose of the play being performed and the roles of which I was supposed to choose one; sometimes I tried to assume one of them and play it, but I would always rattle off the prescribed part parrot fashion, with distaste and a sense of awkwardness and embarrassment. Eventually it totally undermined my feeble performance, so that I preferred to fall silent and retreat to a corner of the stage – and yet up to that moment

I had been in constant fear of throwing away the script and exiting to the darkness of the wings. I used to exit but would still regard my exit as my last role, the role that would eventually, in some strange way, involve me in the play after all.

Now I knew that the other city can only be entered by someone who leaves in the awareness that the journey he is undertaking has no purpose, because purpose means a place in the fabric of relations that create the home, and that it is not even purposeless, because purposelessness simply complements purpose and belongs to his world. The restlessness engendered by the awareness that all testimonies about the other city contradict each other had vanished.

I realized that my efforts to unify my nocturnal interpretations in the light of day were simply the expression of a yearning to incorporate the other city into a familiar order, to change it into a colony of the home, and thereby subjugate and annihilate it. The insoluble question was solved by ceasing to be a question. I now glimpsed in the darkness a space in which alien luminescent shapes rolled around and metamorphosed, shapes that could not be converted to forms from our world and which had no meaning, even though they did contain some kind of justification, which seemed more powerful, authentic and incontrovertible than the justification of meaning: it was a right that was directly connate with being; it was independent and unaccountable to anything, and therefore in danger from nothing. What surged languidly in that space was also a raw presence and cause: a mesmeric and indifferent dark effulgence. The questions I had previously directed at those rolling shapes and to which I had always received different and contradictory answers could not cope with that dark effulgence. In the space that opened up it was impossible to distinguish the sources of the laws and customs from the fragments of extinct beings and detritus of our world, the shapelessness of the beginning from the shapelessness of extinction, the battle of hostile forces from a profound and unshakable unity, turbulent chaos from the most stable order. This space had finally freed itself from the power of home. There opened before me the landscape that they try to protect us from throughout our lives, denying us the right to defeat and the right to exile, the right to lose ourselves and stray alongside walls, to be exiles in the world of nooks and crannies, in the dark courtyards of being. How tedious they are, importunately forcing refuge and home onto us all the time. They want to deprive us of the shining foreign land, where splendid, cold light flows softly from liberated things, of the joy of solitude on nocturnal plains above glittering cities, of the beautiful, slow dance of monsters on a deserted road, of intoxicating extinction in the depth of dark bedrooms, beneath cold mirrors, in which there sway the lights of distant lamps like painful constellations of the zodiacal belt winding through the interior of houses.

I got dressed and dashed down the steps into the street. It was a bright, frosty morning, and the sunlight threw the brows of passersby, the folds of the stone drapery of statues and the snowy ledges into sharp relief. The faces and movements of people I met had already here an expression of dreamy and festive torpor. I walked along narrow lanes plunged in shadow, lanes that suddenly opened onto dazzling squares. I walked through dark colonnades, in whose arches snow shone and scorched tired eyes. I thought about hidden battles, religious services and balls taking place in the depths behind the silent façades, about distant routes into the heart of Asia, of which these streets are part; when I past the memorial to Jan Hus I imagined its hollow interior and wondered what was hidden inside it – was there a wine cellar with a dance floor, a workshop with humming machines, or a swimming pool with the light of colored lamps hanging from the hollow heads of the statues shining on its surface? Maybe today I'll already be swimming lazily in its tepid water, in the flickering patches of light. My body will be caressed by the long tresses of girls who were transported from their families by the marble streetcar and have already forgotten that there exists another world outside the hollow statues. I knew that everyone would talk about failure and desertion. But my departure to the other city was not to be a performance that concealed failure. The pain of defeat had not abated but had strangely merged with the great joy of the journey and become part of it. Escape is the expression used mostly by those who escape every day into the refuge of the home from the summons that wafts from the dark fringes and from the mouths of by-roads. I did not reproach them for taking refuge in the home; there was something admirable and worthy of respect about their loyalty to the play being performed. But nor did I feel the need to apologize to anyone for not performing in their play. Some stay, some leave. Some spend their whole lives unaware of the music of rustles and whispers that accompany our words, while others are absorbed by the patterns on a carpet or the intoxicating interiors of closets – their families sit for several weeks by the open closet door awaiting their return but then they all forget about them. How much longer will the community resent those who leave? When will come the day of reconciliation between those who go and those who stay? When will the departures to the other city turn into quiet celebrations; when will there be no more mocking of those who refused to play or were unable to learn? When will they stop pressing into performance those who already have a rendezvous by the large brick buildings at the freight depot with a green angel whose face is covered in a gold mask? The community doesn't realize how much it needs those who cross the frontier. Those who depart no longer think of the traces they leave behind them in their homeland, and yet for those who remain the departures are a reminder of another space, a reminder that sets the established order quivering and awakes for a while the sleeping force that secretly builds the order and enlivens it: without those who depart the order of the home would become rigid and die. Departure does not mean breaking off the discourse. In fact true discourse is only possible between those who have left and those who remain. Conversations with members of one's tribe are always only a tedious echo of one's own words. All conversations are fed from the great conversation between those who live within the homeland and what wafts over the border: a murmur, in which the rustle of fabric mingles with the howling and whining of monsters and musical compositions played by an orchestra of exiles for the space of several days. Those who live inside regard the voices of the fringes as merely a meaningless verbal accompaniment, to which they pay no attention. Nevertheless those quiet tones and distant cries have a latent effect, eating away the shapes as they withdraw into themselves, ripening at the bottom of memory and bearing fruit.

I crossed Mánes Bridge and walked along by the snow-covered terraced gardens. I had no thought of return but I couldn't have said with certainty that I would never return. I dropped the future from my web of plans; it now glowed with a light, which, in a world where it was our servant, was dim. I had no idea what to expect, whether my sojourn in the other city would be the final denial of the game of home, or instead its renewal and purification in a forgotten fire. It didn't concern me; I abandoned myself to the power of the journey and didn't know whether in the future the journey would command me to remain outside the walls, or to return with my knapsack full of tongues cut from the maws of dragons. What we used to call the future no longer existed, in fact. There was simply a pure and single flame of time; there was just the glow of what was, a glow in which the maturing juices of past events and shapes and the dubious stench of quietly approaching monsters trembled darkly. I climbed the steep lanes alongside the rearmost wings of palaces. I was in no hurry; I had no idea which direction I would take at the next corner. I wondered what employment I would find in the other city: would I be a gold prospector in the jungle of books, a monk in a monastery located in the attic of an apartment house in Libeň, a fisherman sailing after a catch in the dark inner sea and seeing in the distance the evening lamps of the bedrooms? I used to imagine fondly that one could spend a vacation in the other city, and then return and write a book about one's stay there. Fine, so I'll leave here my book about meetings and the frontier. My future books will be written in the script of the other city and printed in nocturnal printing houses hidden behind coats in closets. Maybe some of my books will find their way onto the shelves of antiquarian bookstores. Maybe someone like me will take shelter from a blizzard or a rainstorm in a bookstore and gaze with wonder as a delicate female hand reaches from the other side to make a space between the volumes on the shelf and slip a book into it: the astonished customer will take out the book and stare at the pages covered in strange signs, before leaning forward and peering into the dark fissure remaining between the books on the shelf, where he will glimpse lights twinkling on a dark surface and smell the odor of stone passages. I cut across deserted Hradčany Square and skirted the Martinitz Palace before turning into the lane of Nový

Svět. I walked along it with its stone wall on one side concealing invisible gardens, then climbed crumbling steps that ran alongside the old brick battlements. There was a glint of streetcar tracks. Behind them the small snow-covered park shone in the sunlight. Shadows of trees waving in the wind moved in the snow. I swept the snow from a park bench and sat down, watching the shadows of the branches move about the glittering snow. A streetcar slowly approached from the Powder Bridge. As it came closer I saw it was of green marble. It stopped just outside the little park and all its doors opened. I got up and walked toward it across the untrodden white snow.

## SELECTED DALKEY ARCHIVE PAPERBACKS

**FOR A FULL LIST OF PUBLICATIONS, VISIT:**
## www.dalkeyarchive.com

# SELECTED DALKEY ARCHIVE PAPERBACKS

FOR A FULL LIST OF PUBLICATIONS, VISIT:
www.dalkeyarchive.com